BOOKS BY
CHARLES DE LINT

The Riddle of the Wren

Moonheart: A Romance

The Harp of the Grey Rose

Mulengro: A Romany Tale

Yarrow: An Autumn Tale

Jack, the Giant Killer

Greenmantle

Wolf Moon

Svaha

The Valley of Thunder

Drink Down the Moon

Ghostwood

Angel of Darkness (as Samuel M. Key)

The Dreaming Place

The Little Country

From a Whisper to a Scream
(as Samuel M. Key)

Spiritwalk

Dreams Underfoot (collection)

Into the Green

I'll Be Watching You (as Samuel M. Key)

The Wild Wood

Memory and Dream

The Ivory and the Horn (collection)

Jack of Kinrowan

Trader

Someplace to be Flying

Moonlight and Vines (collection)

Forests of the Heart

Triskell Tales:
22 Years of Chapbooks (collection)

The Road to Lisdoonvarna

The Onion Girl

Seven Wild Sisters
(illustrated by Charles Vess)

A Handful of Coppers (collection)

Waifs and Strays (collection)

Tapping the Dream Tree (collection)

A Circle of Cats (illustrated by Charles Vess)

Spirits in the Wires

Medicine Road (illustrated by Charles Vess)

The Blue Girl

Quicksilver and Shadow (collection)

The Hour Before Dawn (collection)

Triskell Tales 2 (collection)

Widdershins

Promises to Keep

Little (Grrl) Lost

Little
(Grrl)
LOST

CHARLES DE LINT

VIKING

VIKING
Published by Penguin Group
Penguin Group (USA) Inc., 345 Hudson Street, New York, New York 10014, U.S.A.
Penguin Group (Canada), 90 Eglinton Avenue East, Suite 700, Toronto, Ontario, Canada M4P 2Y3
(a division of Pearson Penguin Canada Inc.)
Penguin Books Ltd, 80 Strand, London WC2R 0RL, England
Penguin Ireland, 25 St Stephen's Green, Dublin 2, Ireland (a division of Penguin Books Ltd)
Penguin Group (Australia), 250 Camberwell Road, Camberwell, Victoria 3124, Australia
(a division of Pearson Australia Group Pty Ltd)
Penguin Books India Pvt Ltd, 11 Community Centre, Panchsheel Park, New Delhi – 110 017, India
Penguin Group (NZ), 67 Apollo Drive, Rosedale, North Shore 0745, Auckland, New Zealand
(a division of Pearson New Zealand Ltd.)
Penguin Books (South Africa) (Pty) Ltd, 24 Sturdee Avenue, Rosebank, Johannesburg 2196, South Africa

Penguin Books Ltd, Registered Offices: 80 Strand, London WC2R 0RL, England

First published in 2007 by Viking, a member of Penguin Group (USA) Inc.

A portion of this book was previously published as the short story "Little (Grrl) Lost" in
Firebirds Rising: An Anthology of Original Science Fiction and Fantasy, edited by Sharyn November
(Firebird, an imprint of Penguin Group (USA) Inc., 2006).

Thanks to Anthony Villafranco of San Antonio for some linguistic help.

3 5 7 9 10 8 6 4 2

Copyright © Charles de Lint, 2007
Cover illustration copyright © Scott Fischer, 2007
All rights reserved

LIBRARY OF CONGRESS CATALOGING-IN-PUBLICATION DATA
De Lint, Charles, date–
Little (grrl) lost / Charles De Lint.
p. cm.
Summary: Fourteen-year-old T.J. and her new friend, sixteen-year-old Elizabeth, a six-inch-high
"Little" with a big chip on her shoulder, help one another as T.J. tries to adjust to her family's move
from a farm to the big city and Elizabeth tries to make her own way in the world.
ISBN 978-0-670-06144-0 (hardcover)
[1. Runaways—Fiction. 2. Size—Fiction. 3. Moving, Household—Fiction.
4. Friendship—Fiction. 5. Fantasy.] I. Title. II. Title: Little girl lost.
PZ7.D33954Lit 2007   [Fic]—dc22   2007014832

Printed in U.S.A.   Set in Centaur   Book design by Nancy Brennan

For Julie & Kenny
with a helping of Joss and green chilies
on the side

~~~~~~

Contents

The Annoying Little • I

The Blues Ain't Nothing But a Girl Six Inches Tall • 35

Don't Call Me Tetty • 83

Viva Vega • 161

If I Had Wings . . . • 219

Things That Explode in the Night • 233

And I Bid You Good Night • 267

Little
(Grrl)
LOST

The Annoying Little

§§§§§§§§

SCRITCH, SCRITCH, SCRITCH.

There it was again.

T.J. had first realized that something was living in the walls when she'd seen the cat staring at the baseboards in her bedroom. It was as though Oscar could see right through the wood, and the plaster behind it.

Back when she still thought it was mice, she kept him out of her bedroom and didn't tell anybody. She liked the idea of mice sharing this new house in a new subdivision with her family. If she mentioned it, the traps would come out, just as they had in the old farmhouse where she'd grown up, and her brother, Derek, would be waving little dead mice under her nose again. Ugh. They were so cute with those big eyes of theirs. But they were also dead and gross.

So, no. Telling anyone that the new house had mice was right out.

Instead, she listened to the scritching at night, while lying in her bed. She'd flick on her bedside light, but of course the sound immediately stopped when she did that. It started up again shortly after the light was turned off, but it was impossible to see anything in her shadowy room—even with the curtains open and light coming in her window from the streetlight outside.

So tonight, after Mom and Dad had come in to say their good nights, she pulled her sleeping bag from under her bed and rolled it out beside the part of the wall where she heard the sound most often. Grabbing her pillow, she'd snuggled into the sleeping bag and waited, almost falling asleep before the now-familiar sound brought her wide awake again.

Scritch, scritch.

Except it wasn't really like the sound of mouse claws running around inside the walls. This close—she leaned her ear right up against the baseboard—it sounded an awful lot like voices. Which was stupid. But then she remembered a story her uncle had told her once about how sometimes, when you heard crows in the forest, they could almost sound like human voices. Like real voices, but distant enough that you just couldn't quite make out what they were saying.

That's what the *scritch*ing sounded like.

Oh, right. Like there were crows living inside the walls.

There were a lot of things she didn't like about this new house in the suburbs, but she didn't think she could logically add wall-dwelling crows to the list.

Distracted, she rolled onto her back and stared at the ceiling. She could obsess for hours on the unfairness of having had to move from their farmhouse outside of Tyson to this stupid subdivision, where everything looked pretty much the same from one street to the next. From one *house* to the next. The first time she'd gone out riding her bike, she'd actually found herself pedaling up the wrong drive-way when she was coming back home. Could you feel more stupid?

So that was a big reason to hate being here.

Nobody was very friendly, either. All the kids pretty much ignored her—when they weren't making fun of her accent. But she could live with that. The friends part wasn't totally bad. Sure, she'd had to leave hers behind, but she and Julie could instant message and e-mail all day long, and Tyson was close enough that they could theoretically take the bus to stay with each other on the weekend, though they hadn't yet.

She didn't need a new best friend because she already had one, thank you very much.

But that wasn't totally good either, because talking by phone and computer couldn't begin to be the same. Not when they used to be able to simply cut across the cornfield and just *be* at each other's house.

She missed that. She missed the farm. She missed driving the tractor and messing about in the barn with Dad's tools and machines. But most of all, she missed Red. Her handsome, sweet-tempered, mischievous Red. He—okay, technically, it, since he'd been gelded—had been the perfect horse, but she'd had to give him up.

That was what was so *totally* unfair.

So, maybe it wasn't her parents' fault. She didn't under-stand much about stock-market crashes, except that if you had your money in the wrong kind of investment, you could end up losing it all when the market fell. Which was what had happened to them.

But shouldn't you be able to see that coming?

Apparently not.

Apparently, you could lose all your savings, and your family home, and have to start over fresh again, where you were supposed to put on a good face, your best foot forward, soldier on. Even when it meant you'd lost the most important thing in your life.

When you hadn't lost so much, dealing with it wasn't so hard. Mom was happy with her new job at the hospital. Dad didn't seem to mind going to an office every day instead of working out of the spare room the way he'd done pretty much forever. Even stupid Derek was happy, because now he was in a place where he could start up a real band and there were clubs where he could play. He already had a bunch of new friends, though obviously no loyalty to old ones the way she did.

Red mattered to her. Julie mattered to her.

Did anyone ever consider *her* feelings? Of course not. She was only fourteen. No one cared about what *she* thought.

It was all, "You'll make new friends."

Like her old ones weren't important.

Or, "We can't afford to board Red, T.J. Maybe in a couple of years we can get you a new horse."

But a new horse wouldn't be Red.

It was all Dad's fault for losing their money.

And Mom's for taking this stupid job—which had

brought them to the city in the first place—and then acting like the change would be good for the whole family.

And Derek's for being so happy to live here.

She could feel the tears welling up behind her eyes like they always did when she thought of her beautiful Red. Like they did when she was "just feeling sorry for herself instead of embracing life's challenges," as Mom would say. Well, she had every reason to feel sorry for herself.

Scritch, scritch.

The sound brought her back. She wiped her sleeve against her eyes and turned to stare at the wall. She wished she had Oscar's apparent X-ray vision, because it really did sound like voices. But now, instead of being curious, she was kind of bored and irritated. She raised her fist to bang on the wall, then froze.

Because the impossible happened.

A small section of the baseboard opened as though it was a tiny door, spilling out a square of light. A girl appeared in the doorway, looking back inside. She held a duffel bag in one hand and was wearing a jean jacket over a T-shirt, a short red-and-black plaid skirt, and clunky black shoes. Her hair was a neon blue. She looked to be about sixteen or seventeen.

And stood about six inches high.

"I'm not that person," she called back to someone inside, her voice hard and angry. "I don't want to be that person. I'm *never* going to be that person, and you can't make me!"

"Tetty Wood, you come back inside this instant!" a voice called from within.

"And my name's not Tetty!" the miniature girl shouted back.

She stepped outside and slammed the baseboard door shut.

The sudden loss of light made T.J. blink in the darkness.

I've fallen asleep, she thought. Fallen asleep and started to dream that action figures can come to life. Because that was what the girl appeared to be. The size of one of Derek's old action figures, complete with duffel-bag accessory.

But her eyes had now adjusted to the low light, and there the miniature girl was. She stared back at T.J., her eyes apparently adjusting at the same time, and suddenly realized that she wasn't alone.

"Oh, crap," she said. "Don't swat me."

T.J. realized that she still had her fist in the air from when she was going to bang it against the wall.

"I thought you were mice," she said, lowering her hand.

"Do I look like a mouse?"

"No, but when I could only hear you . . ."

T.J.'s voice trailed off. She felt stupid, like she did too much of the time since they'd left the farm. And why should she? People supposedly got that way when they were nervous or scared—according to her father—but she was a hundred times bigger than this uninvited guest glaring up at her. What did she have to be scared about?

And it was *her* bedroom.

"So what *is* your name?" she asked.

It seemed the most polite question. Better than, What *are* you and why are you living inside my bedroom walls?

"Elizabeth."

"But whoever was inside—"

"My uptight parents."

"—called you Tetty."

"It's a stupid nickname. *Their* stupid nickname. My name's Elizabeth."

"I'm Tara Jane Moore, but most people call me T.J." She waited a moment, then added, "I like having a nickname."

"Whatever works for you," Elizabeth said.

She'd dropped her duffel bag to the floor and stood looking up at T.J. with her hands on her hips, a challenge in her eyes.

"So what's your damage?" she asked.

"I'm sorry?"

"For what?"

"I meant, what do you mean?" T.J. said.

Elizabeth gave a wave of her tiny hand. "Why are you sleeping on the floor when you've got a perfectly good bed?"

"I was curious about the noises I was hearing . . ."

Elizabeth laughed. "See, they've got this huge worry thing going on. 'Don't be seen.' 'Always stay hidden.' But it turns out that all their yelling was just *attracting* attention."

"You mean your parents?"

"Oh, yeah. There's, like, a hundred rules and regs, and they've been drilling them into us since the day we were born."

T.J. nodded. She knew all about strict parents. Like the kind who just gave away your horse and moved you to some ugly subdivision, and then expected you to be happy about it.

She peered more closely at Elizabeth.

"So, do you have wings?" she asked.

"Do you see wings?"

"No. I just thought they might be folded up under your jacket."

"Why would I have wings?"

"Well, aren't you a fairy?"

"Oh, please. I'm a Little."

"I can see that."

"No, it's like you saying you're a human being. A Little's what I am."

"I don't think I'd ever say that. Who goes around saying they're a human being, except maybe the Elephant Man?"

"Whatever." Elizabeth cocked her head, reminding T.J. of a bird. "So you're okay with a little person just showing up in your bedroom like this?"

"I suppose I shouldn't be—I mean, it's totally unreal, isn't it?—but I don't feel surprised at all, and I don't know why."

Elizabeth nodded. "And the 'rents get all in a twist about anyone even guessing that we exist. I knew it would be no big deal."

"Well, it *could* be a big deal," T.J. said.

"How do you figure?"

"Think about it. If the world found out someone like you is real, it'd be all over the news."

"Cool. I'm so ready for my fifteen minutes of fame. Look out, world, 'cause here I come."

"I don't think it would be like that. I think it'd be more like they'd put you in a terrarium in a laboratory to study you. And everybody'd be tearing up their baseboards looking for more of you." She paused for a moment before adding, "Do you have, like, a house back there?"

"Oh, sure. It's just all small and secret, you know, and it stretches out through the walls. But we've got all the amenities. We only moved here a few years ago, when they first built these houses, but it's totally comfortable now. My brothers and I even dragged in an old miniature TV that we found in the garage and hooked it up to the cable. It's, like, totally big screen for us."

"So why do you want to leave?" T.J. asked. "I mean, that's what you're doing, right? Running away?"

"I'm not running. I'm old enough to make my own decisions about my life."

"You don't look much older than me."

"I'm sixteen."

"That's not old enough to live on your own."

"My mother was already married and had her first kid when she was my age."

"Gross."

Elizabeth shrugged. "It's no biggie." She looked around the room. "So, do you mind if I crash here with you tonight? I'd kind of like to avoid going outside until it starts to get light."

She might be two years older than me, T.J. thought, but at least I'm not afraid of the dark.

"I like it outside at night," T.J. said. "Sometimes I sneak out and just sit and look at the sky for a while, but it's not the same here as it was back home. The sky's way duller."

"That's because of the light pollution from the city. And I'm not scared of the dark."

"Then why won't you go out at night?"

"I didn't say I couldn't. It's just not safe with cats and owls and foxes and all."

"Oh, right."

"So, are you staying here on the floor? Because I want to bed down somewhere that you won't roll over on me in the middle of the night."

"No, of course not."

T.J. threw her pillow onto the bed and got up, being careful not to drop the flap of her sleeping bag on the Little or step in her direction.

"I'm going to put on the light for a minute," she said. "Is that okay?"

"It's your room. Knock yourself out."

The bright glare blinded both of them. Blinking, T.J. went over to her dresser and took her old teddy bear out of the little stuffed chair it was sitting in. She put the chair on her night table, then turned to Elizabeth.

"You can use this," she said. "I guess it's big enough to be a couch for you."

"Thanks."

"Do you want a hand up?"

Elizabeth gave her withering look. "Do I look like a cripple?"

"No, it's just . . ."

T.J.'s voice trailed off as Elizabeth opened her duffel bag and took out a length of rope with a hook on the end. The hook folded out into three prongs so that it looked like an anchor. After a couple of swings over her head, up it went, catching in the cloth of the comforter at the top of the bed. She gave the rope an experimental tug. When she was satisfied it would hold her weight, she slung her duffel onto her back, using its handles as straps, and shimmied up the rope.

"Wow," T.J. said. "You're strong. I am so useless trying to do ropes in gym."

Elizabeth grinned, pleased at having impressed her.

"We learn how to get around at an early age," she said.

She worked the hook out of the comforter and coiled the rope, then walked across the top of the bed and jumped over to the night table. It was only a few inches, but when T.J. worked out the proportions, she realized it would be like her jumping over a gap as wide as her own height.

Elizabeth acted like it was no big deal. Dumping her duffel and the rope on the top of the night table, she stretched out on the chair. It wasn't quite a couch for her, but easily big enough that she could lounge comfortably in it.

T.J. got into bed and lay down with her head facing her guest.

"I still can't believe you're real," she said.

"Get used to it. The world's a big and strange place, my

dad says, and just because you haven't seen a thing doesn't mean it doesn't exist."

"Obviously."

It was funny. Elizabeth acted like she hated her parents, but when she'd mentioned her dad just now, she seemed kind of proud of him.

"Will they come looking for you?" she asked. "Your parents?"

"I doubt it. They'll be totally freaking right now that you've seen me. They're probably packing up and moving the whole family out as we speak."

"They don't have to do that. I won't tell anyone."

"That doesn't mean anything to them. You could promise on whatever you care for the most, and they figure you'll tell anyway. 'Don't trust a Big.' That's, like, one of the major rules."

T.J. was insulted.

"Hey, don't look so bummed. It's not personal. That's just what they believe. And it's worse 'cause you're a kid, and in the world of my parents, kids only do what they're supposed to when you keep them under your thumb. God forbid you should have a thought of your own."

"Yeah, I know that feeling."

"So that's your horse?" Elizabeth asked, hooking a thumb in the direction of the picture of Red, which shared the night table with her chair and a small lamp.

"*Was* my horse."

"Yeah, I've heard you arguing with your parents about it. That sucks." She shook her head. "You know, it's funny, you thinking we were mice, because I had a pet mouse once. His name was Reggie."

A sweet-sad look came into her eyes, and T.J. realized that this was the first time Elizabeth's features had softened. Up until that moment, she'd worn a look of steady confrontation, as though everything in the world was her enemy and she had to stand up against all of it.

"What happened to him?" she asked.

"Same as what happened to you. My parents made me get rid of him."

"But why?"

"Well, you know mice. They just poop and pee whenever they have to, no matter where they are. You can't train them. I'd take him out with me when we were foraging—for his exercise and the company. The 'rents said that his pellets would make the Bigs think their house was infested with mice and they'd call in an exterminator or something, and then where would we be?"

"I like mice," T.J. said, feeling a little guilty for all the ones that had been trapped and killed back on the farm.

"What's not to like? Besides the pooping and peeing, I mean. I promised to clean up after him—like they cared or believed me. But I would have." She sighed, then added, "I loved that old fellow. I really did. I think that's when I started to hate my parents."

"You don't really hate them."

"Don't I?" She had that hard look on her face again. "I'm surprised you don't hate yours—considering what they did."

T.J. thought about that. Her parents exasperated her, and she was still upset for what they'd done, but she didn't hate them. How could you hate your own parents?

"I just don't," she said.

"Whatever."

"So, are you really going to go out into the world and let everyone know you exist?"

"No, I'm not crazy. I know it would be a horror show. When you're my size, being secret and sneaking around is about all you've got going for you. A Big could just smash me like a bug, and there wouldn't be anything I could do about it."

"So, what are you going to do?"

She shrugged. "I don't know. Get away from here and find someplace to live, I guess. Someplace snug, where I can have a mouse if I want one."

"You could stay here," T.J. said. "I don't know if having a mouse is the greatest idea, but I could get you a bunch of little furniture and sneak you food and stuff."

"Oh, so I could be your pet?"

"No, nothing like that. I just thought it would be fun and, you know, safe for you."

Elizabeth shook her head. "Not going to happen. Don't take this personally, but you're a little too Goody Two-shoes for my tastes, and anyway, the whole purpose of going out on my own is to prove that I can do it."

T.J. would have felt insulted about being called Goody Two-shoes, except she knew she was. She did what she was told and tried to do well in school. She kept her blonde hair cut to her shoulders, and she would never have worn a skirt as short as Elizabeth's.

"But who are you going to be proving it to if your family moves away?" she asked.

"That's a dumb question," Elizabeth told her.

But she had a funny look in her eyes as she said it—there for a moment, then quickly gone.

"You should turn out the light," she said. "I'd like to get some sleep before I take off in the morning."

"Okay."

T.J. reached for the light switch, then paused before turning the light off.

"I probably won't be awake when you go," she said. "I'm not much of a morning person anymore. So, good luck and, you know, everything. I hope you find a way to be happy."

"Soon as I'm out of here, I'll be happy."

"And if you want to leave your family a note or something—to let them know that I really won't tell, I mean—you should, so that they won't move."

"Like they'd ever listen."

"Um, right. Well, good night."

"Sure. Can you get that light?"

T.J. flicked the switch, and the room plunged into darkness.

Just before she fell asleep, she thought she heard Elizabeth say softly, "But just because you're a Goody Two-shoes, doesn't mean I don't think you're okay."

But maybe that was only because it was something she wanted to hear.

~~~~~~

T.J. awoke to find that Saturday had started much earlier without her; the sun was already well above the horizon. She looked at her night table. There was no Little sleeping in her teddy's stuffed armchair. There was no Little anywhere to be seen, nor any sign that there'd ever been one.

That's because you were dreaming, she told herself.

But it certainly felt as though it had been real.

She lay in bed remembering the punky six-inch-tall Elizabeth, with her neon-blue hair and enough attitude for a half dozen full-size girls.

It would have been cool if she had been real.

After a while, T.J. got up and turned on her computer. While she waited for it to boot up, she knelt on the floor where, in her dream, a door had opened in the baseboard. She couldn't see any sign of it now—except for maybe *there*. But that was probably only where one board had ended and another had been laid in.

When she returned to her computer, she went online and Googled the word *Little*. Her screen cleared, and then the first ten entries of 215 million appeared.

Well, that hadn't been a particularly good idea.

She tried refining the search by adding *people* and got links to toy lines, the Little People of America site, an archeological news report on the finding of the remains of a miniature woman on an island in Indonesia—except since her head was the size of a grapefruit, she wasn't exactly tiny. T.J. scrolled through a few more pages, but nothing was useful, even if there were only some forty-seven million hits this time.

"Little magical people" got her thirty-seven hits that were closer to what she was looking for, but nothing that resembled Elizabeth.

What? she asked herself. You were expecting something from a dream to show up on the Net?

She tried "Littles," and that was no help, either.

Finally, she tried "little people living behind the baseboards" and was surprised when something came up—a site called "Fairies, Ghosts and Monsters." It sounded pretty Game Boy–useless, but she clicked through anyway. It turned out to be run by a professor who used to teach at one of the local universities and contained an odd mix of stories and scholarly essays.

She found the "Littles" a few pages in, under "miniature secret people." The article cited literary references like *Gulliver's Travels* and *Mistress Masham's Repose*, the Borrowers of Mary Norton's books, Brownies from a Sunday comic strip that was long gone, a series of books actually called "The Littles," and the Smalls from a book written by some old English guy named William Dunthorn.

There were two anecdotal entries, both about little people who lived behind the baseboards. One talked about "pennymen," who turned into pennies when people looked their way. And then there were the Littles. The way they were described seemed very close to what Elizabeth had told her. There was even a children's picture book about them: *The Travelling Littles*, written and illustrated by someone named Sheri Piper, who, like the professor whose Web site this was, lived in town.

According to Piper's book, Littles had originally been birds who got too lazy to fly on after they'd found a particularly good feed. Eventually, they lost their wings and became these little people who had to live by their wits, taking up residence in people's houses, where they foraged for food and whatever else they needed.

She Googled the author, but the only links that came up were to eBay and used-book stores. Apparently, the book was long out of print, although she had written a number of others. None of those seemed to be about Littles. At least, she couldn't tell from the few links she clicked on to get more information.

She made a note of the author's name and the title of the one relevant book so that she could look them up at the library, then went to have a shower and some breakfast.

When she came into the kitchen, her mother was just about to let Oscar out the back door.

"Don't let him out!" T.J. cried.

What if he came upon Elizabeth's scent and tracked her down to where she was hiding?

Her *imaginary* scent, the logical part of her corrected.

"Why ever not?" her mother asked.

"Because . . . I . . . I want to brush him first."

Her mother gave her a look that said, "When have you *ever* willingly brushed the cat?"

"Can you just leave him in?" T.J. asked. "Just until I've had breakfast and can brush him."

"Stop you from taking on a responsibility?" her mother said. "Not this mom."

"Ha ha."

But her mother left the cat inside. Oscar complained at the door, then shot T.J. a dirty look as though he was well aware of who was responsible for his lack of freedom before he stalked off down the hall.

T.J. poured herself some orange juice and took a box of cereal from the cupboard before joining her mother at the kitchen table.

"We're almost out of milk," her mother said. "Better use it before your dad gets up and takes it for his coffee."

"I will."

"What has you up so early? Surely not just to brush the cat."

Saturday morning everyone in the house slept in except for T.J.'s mother. Back on the farm, T.J. had gotten up early, too, but she didn't have Red to look after anymore, and so had gotten into the habit of staying up late at night and sleeping in as long as possible.

T.J. shrugged. "Maybe I'm turning over a new leaf."

"Well, I'm happy for the company."

T.J. shook cereal into her bowl. She looked over at her mother as she reached for the milk.

"So, when you were a kid," she said, "did anyone ever take something away from you that you really, really cared about?"

Her mother sighed. "Please, T.J. I know you feel terrible

about having to give up Red. Believe it or not, *I* feel terrible about it, too. But we have to move on."

"No, I didn't mean that. I was wondering about *you*. What did you do? How did you move on?"

Did you make up imaginary six-inch-high Littles to help you cope? she added to herself.

"Why are you asking me this?"

"I don't know. I . . ."

T.J. knew she couldn't talk about the Littles. For one thing, she'd promised not to. For another, her mom would think she was nuts. So she improvised.

"It's just there was this girl in the park yesterday," she said, "and we got to talking about . . . you know, stuff. And it turns out she was running away from home because she hates her parents, and the reason she hates them—or at least the main one, I guess—is that they made her get rid of her . . . um, pet dog that she'd had forever. So I was wondering—"

"What's her name?" her mother asked. "We need to tell her parents."

"*Mom.* We can't do that. It's not our business."

Her mother shook her head. "Sometimes we have to involve ourselves in other people's lives, whether they want us to or not."

"Well, I don't know anything about her. I don't even know if she lives around here. I just met her in the park, and she was already on her way."

"T.J., this is serious."

"I know. But it's something that's already done, and that wasn't the point of it anyway."

Her mother studied her for a moment.

"Do you hate us?" she asked.

T.J. shook her head. "I get mad whenever I think of how you made me lose Red, but . . . I don't know. It's not like it'd make me hate you."

"Thank God for that."

"Not like I hate living here."

"We've been through the why of it a hundred times."

"I know. I was just mentioning it, since you brought it up."

Her mother gave her a look.

"Okay," T.J. said. "So I did. But you still didn't answer my question."

"What exactly are you worried about?"

"That I'll end up hating you like this Elizabeth does her parents. So that's why I was wondering if something like this had ever happened to you."

"No," her mother said. "It never did. And don't think either your father or I are even remotely happy that things have turned out this way. We know how much you loved that horse."

"Red. His name's Red."

T.J. had to look down at her cereal and blink back the start of tears. Her mother's hand reached across the table and held hers.

"I know, sweetheart," she said. "I really am so sorry."

"I guess."

"And I don't think you'll start hating us—at least I hope to God you won't, because that would be just too much to bear. But if we can still have a talk like this, then I think we're okay."

Except they weren't, T.J. thought. At least she wasn't.

She didn't hate her parents. But that didn't help the big hole in her chest where Red used to be.

T.J. dutifully brushed Oscar after breakfast—a chore that neither of them appreciated very much—then reluctantly, she let him outside. Surely, Elizabeth would have taken cats into account and hidden herself away in some place where they wouldn't be able to find her. Assuming Elizabeth was even real.

And speaking of real . . . once she'd closed the door behind the cat, she went up to her room and knelt down by the wall where last night a little door had opened in the baseboard.

"I don't know if you're still in there," she said, "or if you can even trust me—but I just want you to know that no matter what happens, your secret's safe with me. I mean, it's not like someone hasn't already written a book about you, and you *can* be looked up on the Web. But I won't add my two cents—not even if someone asks me, point-blank. I already lied to my mother about you, and I hated having to do that. I've never done it before. But that's how seriously I take keeping my word."

There was no reply.

Well, she hadn't exactly been expecting one. It was just something she felt she'd needed to say.

A week went by, and then another. T.J. didn't hear any more noises behind the baseboards. She didn't see any little people, or even signs of them. She did find *The Travelling Littles* at the library and read it. The book didn't tell her any more than she'd already known from Elizabeth and the Web site. It was kind of a little-kids' story, but she liked the artwork. The Littles in the pictures were old fashioned, but old fashioned in an interesting way.

Goody Two-shoes, she remembered Elizabeth saying.

Maybe she should get a new haircut—something cooler.

She laughed at the thought. Right. Get a makeover because of a put-down by an imaginary, miniature girl.

But that was the odd thing about it. Although she was about 95 percent sure she'd just dreamed the whole business, the memory of it didn't go away the way dreams usually did. She kept finding herself worrying about Elizabeth, out there in the big world on her own. And what about her family? What had happened to them? Had they moved? They must have moved, because it was so quiet behind the walls now. Even Oscar had stopped staring at the baseboards.

But maybe they were just being really, *really* careful now.

They had some of Sheri Piper's other books in the library, and she was surprised to find a second book about the Littles. It was called *Mr. Pennyinch's Wings* and was about how the Littles regained their ability to turn into birds. She wondered if Elizabeth and her family knew about it.

Of course, it was just a book. That didn't mean the story was real.

It didn't even mean Littles were real. Just that someone was writing about them.

She was true to her word and never said anything to anyone. The only time she felt guilty was when she was talking on the phone to Julie. They'd never had secrets before, and now she had a Big One.

Maybe this was what happened when best friends were separated by distance. You started keeping things to yourself, then you started calling each other less. And then finally, you stopped being best friends. She hoped that wasn't going to happen, but there'd already been a day last week when she hadn't phoned or messaged Julie.

The thought made her feel sad and sent her into a whole blue mood that started with Julie and took her all the way back to the memory of the day they'd had to walk Red into the horse trailer and take him to his new home.

The closest she came to telling Julie was a week after she'd had her encounter with Elizabeth, when they were on the phone.

"Have you ever seen a fairy?" T.J. found herself asking.

"Oh, sure. Duncan's father is supposed to be one."

"Really?"

"That's what Melissa told me. But you shouldn't call them that. Just say they're gay."

"No, I meant a real fairy."

Julie started to laugh. "What, with little wings and everything? God, what's that city doing to you? I thought only country bumpkins like me were supposed to believe in things like that."

"I still feel like a bumpkin."

"Does that mean *you* believe in fairies?" Julie asked.

Elizabeth hadn't had wings, T.J. thought, so technically, she couldn't be considered a fairy and there was no need to lie.

"Of course I don't," she said.

"So, are there *any* cute guys there or what?"

"There's lots of cute guys. They just never think *I'm* cute."

"The dummies."

"Totally."

T.J. had taken to brushing Oscar on a regular basis.

It had started out as a continuation of her cover-up that first morning when Elizabeth had run away, but now they'd both come to enjoy it. T.J. would sit with Oscar out on the back porch, where the view of the one maple and three spruce in the yard let her pretend she was still back on the farm. At least, it worked if she looked up into their branches, instead of across at the neighbor's backyard.

She'd hold the cat on her lap and brush him with long, gentle strokes, carefully working out the mats. Oscar would soon start purring, and T.J. would slip into the same sort of contemplative mood that used to come over her when she was currying Red.

She was staring dreamily off into space one morning, hand on a sleeping Oscar, the brushing long finished, when her brother, Derek, interrupted her.

"Hey, dufus," he said. "Still playing with dolls?"

When she looked up, he tossed something at her. She caught it before she could see what it was, startling Oscar, who bolted across the lawn.

"You are such a moron," she started to tell him.

But then she looked at the small duffel bag she held in her hand, and she could feel her face go pale. Luckily, Derek didn't appear to notice.

"Where did you get this?" she asked him, standing up.

"In the shed. Or should we start calling it the dolly house?"

"In the shed?"

"Yeah. I needed to replace the brake on my in-line skates and was looking for my spare. That thing fell off a shelf when I was moving some boxes around. What were *you* doing in there with your dollies?"

"Nothing."

He cocked his head, then asked, "So it's not yours?"

"Did you look inside it?"

"Sure. It's full of doll clothes."

Of course it would seem that way, T.J. thought. It belonged to Elizabeth. Who was real. How long had she been living in the shed? Was she even still there? Had Derek crushed her, moving around boxes?

Derek was still looking at her. To cover for Elizabeth, T.J. swallowed her pride.

"Of course it's mine. I was just . . . you know . . ."

Derek laughed. "Nope, I don't. And I don't want to, either."

He grinned at her and walked off, shaking his head.

She waited until he'd gone around the side of the house and into the garage, then ran for the shed. It was hard to see in there, shadows deepening the farther she looked. It had that smell she'd always enjoyed—machinery and the gas for the mower—and reminded her of the barn back home.

"Elizabeth?" she called softly. "Are you in here?"

There was no answer.

Oh, God. She'd been eaten by a cat. Or a . . . a weasel or something.

"Elizabeth, please say something."

She looked everywhere, but there was nobody to be found. Especially not a six-inch Little with bright blue hair.

It was all T.J. could think about for the rest of the day.

She went back into the shed twice more with no better luck. That night, lying in bed, she couldn't stand it. She certainly couldn't sleep. So she got dressed, found a flashlight, and went back out to the shed once more, the little duffel bag stuck in the pocket of her jacket.

She'd never been afraid of the dark, but it was spookier than she liked at the back of the yard. The shed door made a loud creak when she opened it, and she stood silent, holding her breath. But no lights came on in the house behind her. Allowing herself to breathe again, she flicked on the flashlight and stepped inside.

The first thing its beam found was a disheveled Elizabeth sitting on a spool of wire on the middle shelf. She blocked the light from her eyes with one hand and frowned.

T.J. aimed the light at the floor.

"Thank God you're okay," she said.

"Piss off."

"What?"

"I said, piss off. I don't need your stupid sympathy. I'm doing just fine, okay?"

"But why are you still here?"

"Maybe I like it here."

T.J. never liked to make trouble or impose where she obviously wasn't wanted. It was what was making it so hard for her to make new friends in the neighborhood and at school. So her first inclination was to leave Elizabeth alone. But then she remembered what her mother had said.

Sometimes we have to involve ourselves in other people's lives, whether they want us to or not.

"I don't think you do," T.J. said. "God, what have you been living on out here?"

She didn't add that it was obvious Elizabeth could really use a bath and a hair wash.

Elizabeth shrugged. "I found an old bag of birdseed and put out a container to catch rainwater."

"You have to come back to the house with me. I'll get you some real food."

"They're gone, aren't they?"

"You mean your family?"

"No, the zits on your butt. Of *course* I mean my family."

"I don't know," T.J. said. "Maybe they're just being really quiet."

"No, they're gone."

"I guess. . . ."

"So what's the point of going back? It would have been horrible going back, having to admit they were right. I *can't* survive out here on my own. But now they're not even there."

"So what's the point of staying out here?" T.J. asked.

Elizabeth shrugged. "It's what I deserve for being such an idiot."

"Now you're just talking stupid."

Elizabeth looked up at her, eyes flashing.

"Remember what I said when you came in?" she asked. "Why don't you just do it? Piss off and leave me alone."

T.J. didn't move.

"Look," Elizabeth said. "You have no idea what it's like being me. Not having friends. Living somewhere you don't want, with people who don't understand you. Okay? So don't pretend *you* understand and can somehow make it better."

"You are so full of crap," T.J. said.

"What?"

"You act so brave, but here you still are, hiding out in my shed."

"You don't think I'd go if I could? But the night's full of owls and cats, and the day's full of hawks and dogs and more cats. The few times I've tried to get away, I almost got eaten alive!"

"So what? You think you're the only person to feel scared

or alone? Do you think I have all kinds of kids falling over me, wanting to be my friend? Do you think I don't miss the farm and Red?"

"At least you're a normal size."

"Oh, yeah. That makes it really easy."

Elizabeth glared at her. "So what's your big point?"

"God, you are such a piece of work," T.J. snapped. "I should just wrap some tape around that big mouth of yours, stick you in a padded envelope, and mail you somewhere."

Elizabeth's eyes widened a little. And then she actually smiled.

"Wow," she said.

"Wow what?"

"You do have some backbone."

T.J. wasn't sure if she should feel complimented or insulted. That old "Goody Two-shoes" comment still rankled.

"Sorry, I wasn't being snarky," Elizabeth added.

"Did I just hear you apologize?"

Elizabeth went on as though T.J. hadn't spoken. "It's just, you go around and let everybody walk all over you."

"I don't. I just like to get along."

"Even if you don't get your way?"

T.J. sighed. "It's not like that. It's not all about getting your own way. Sometimes there's a bigger picture. Sure, I hate that we moved. And I really, really hated having to give up Red. But we're still a family, and things had to change because . . . because they just did. It wasn't anybody's fault. It's just how it worked out."

"So you just go along with it?"

"Yes. No. I don't know. I'm trying to make the best of it, okay? Which is more than I can say for you. All you do is go around with a big chip on your shoulder. How does that make it better for you or anybody around you?"

"You're probably right."

T.J. blinked in surprise. "I am?"

Elizabeth shrugged. "Well, look where it's got me so far."

Neither of them said anything for a long moment.

"Do you want to come back to the house?" T.J. finally asked.

"I guess."

"We could try to find your family," T.J. went on. "Or some other Littles. I could carry you so that you don't have to worry about being attacked or anything."

"Like a pet."

T.J. rolled her eyes. "No, like a friend."

"I guess. . . ."

"You know there's books about Littles."

Elizabeth nodded. "One, at least. None of us can figure out how she got the story so right."

"She's written a new one."

Elizabeth raised her eyebrows.

"It's about how the Littles have learned to turn back into birds. You know, like werewolves or something. They can just go back and forth, and they don't even have to wait for a full moon."

"No way."

T.J. shrugged. "Well, it's just a book."

"Yeah, but her other one was dead-on."

"So maybe we could look her up. She lives here—or at least in the city."

Elizabeth got up and brushed the dust from her very short, very dirty skirt. It didn't do much good.

"I *am* kind of hungry," she said. "For real food, I mean."

"We've got plenty."

"And I'm dying to be clean again."

"We've got water, too."

Elizabeth nodded. "So . . . thanks, T.J. I guess I'll take you up on your hospitality."

"Do you . . . um, want to go under your own steam?"

"Instead of being carried like a pet?"

"It wouldn't be—"

Elizabeth smiled. "I know. I'm just pushing your buttons. Actually, I'd appreciate the lift."

T.J. laid her hand palm-up on the shelf beside the Little. When Elizabeth climbed on, she carefully cupped her hand a little and stuck up a finger for Elizabeth to hang on to. Elizabeth didn't hesitate to use it.

"So where does this writer live again?" she asked as T.J. lifted her into the air.

"The librarian said somewhere downtown."

"I wonder how hard she'd be to find?"

"Shh," T.J. told her as she stepped out of the shed. "You're supposed to be a secret, remember?"

"Maybe you could mail me to her."

"Shh."

"But in a box. With padding and air holes . . ."

"Really, you need to shush."

"Can't you just imagine her face when she opens it and out I pop?"

"*Shh.*"

But they couldn't stop giggling softly as they made their way back into the house.

The Blues Ain't Nothing But a Girl Six Inches Tall

ﻆﻆﻆﻆﻆﻆﻆ

T.J. SHOULD HAVE known that it would be impossible to keep Elizabeth a secret forever.

She wasn't so worried about Derek bursting into her room unannounced. These days he only seemed to be at home to sleep and for the occasional meal. The rest of the time he was out with his new friends. Studying at their houses, practicing with the band that a few of them were putting together, hanging down at the parking lot of the twenty-four-hour Stop'n'Go on the Strip—which was the only place nearby that kids could gather, except for the community park. But the cool kids didn't go there.

From things she'd overheard in school, and the tidbits that Derek would drop from time to time when it was just the two of them in the house, she knew all about what the kids got up to down on the Strip.

They preferred to play cat-and-mouse with the security guards who patrolled the checkerboard of parking lots. They weren't particularly hard or tough kids, but they smoked and drank beer. They raced their cars, always staying one step ahead of the security guards, and some of them did a variety of drugs to a soundtrack of hip-hop, rap, and electronica.

Derek and his friends were on the periphery of this crowd and preferred a punkier, bluesy sound. The soundtrack to their lives was more along the lines of the Libertines and Green Day, Led Zeppelin, Jimi Hendrix and the White Stripes. Derek's friend Brad had a car, so they did cruise the Strip from time to time, but they spent most of their weekends practicing music—which was a good thing, because so far, T.J. thought their band sucked. The only good thing about them was their lead singer, a black guy named Reg who seemed to be channeling Robert Plant or Jack White and had no patience for people who assumed that just because he was black he should be singing soul or rapping.

Elizabeth was fascinated with the band and hid in the rec room whenever they were practicing at T.J.'s house so that she could listen to them. She also tried to convince T.J. to take her to the Strip, but T.J. wouldn't even discuss it after the first few times Elizabeth brought it up. Elizabeth would probably fit right in if she were the size of a normal girl, but what were they going to do, considering the way things were? No thanks.

Besides, while T.J.'s parents gave Derek freer rein, there was no way they'd let T.J. hang around on the Strip.

T.J.'s parents were also a bigger problem in terms of her hiding Elizabeth. After last year, they'd proven that they couldn't be trusted with anything really important, but at least they did call out or knock before they came into the room. That was enough warning for Elizabeth to duck out of sight, and the two girls always made sure to keep their voices down, or T.J. played music so that no one could hear them. But T.J.'s mother noticed that food was missing whenever T.J. foraged for Elizabeth, and T.J. knew that she always looked guilty when one of her parents appeared in her room. While she didn't think they thought she was doing drugs, they knew she was hiding something.

But the real problem was Oscar.

For Oscar, anything smaller than him was fair game— and occasionally larger creatures, too, such as when some dog decided to invade his personal space. It took forever to convince him that Elizabeth was neither a toy nor food, and even then, when T.J. went to school, Elizabeth had to retreat back into the rooms between the walls that her family had abandoned. There was no way T.J. could trust Oscar when she wasn't around.

Naturally, Elizabeth complained about all of this: having to hide, not getting to do anything interesting, having to be careful around Oscar. T.J. and Elizabeth might have bonded that night in the garden shed, quietly giggling and talking long into the early hours of the morning when they got back to T.J.'s room, and they got along much better than they had the first night they met, but Elizabeth could still be cranky and sarcastic, and had greater expectations of T.J. than T.J. knew she could ever live up to.

It wasn't just T.J.'s refusal to go to the Strip, or do *"any-thing* even *remotely* interesting" so that Elizabeth could at least live vicariously through her. The Little also didn't think T.J. was doing nearly enough in implementing their plan to contact Sheri Piper, the author of *The Travelling Littles*.

But it wasn't easy to actually do.

To start with, there was no listing for Sheri Piper in the phone book. She didn't have a Web site, either, so there was no way to contact her except through her publisher. At least, that's what Ms. Stewart, the school librarian, said when T.J. asked her how it could be done.

T.J. had never written to an author before, but she could imagine how well her questions would go over. Piper would think she was some crazed fan who couldn't tell the difference between real and make-believe. She probably wouldn't even answer. And even if she *did* answer, it would be only to write something noncommittal, like "Thanks for your interest."

She probably got tons of letters.

She probably didn't even read her own fan mail.

T.J. sighed. This felt way too complicated already, and they hadn't even started.

"We'll just have to find her the old-fashioned way," Elizabeth said.

T.J. glanced at where the Little sat in her overstuffed chair beside the computer monitor, hidden from anyone suddenly stepping in from the doorway. She was wearing a pair of snug-fitting jeans and a T-shirt on which she'd written LITTLE BOYS SUCK with a marker pen.

"And what way is that?" T.J. asked.

Elizabeth shrugged. "You know. Do some detective work."

"I wouldn't know where to start."

"I do. I've seen all the TV shows. You just stake out her publisher's offices, and then, when she comes out, you follow her home."

"It's not that simple," T.J. said.

"It is if you let it be."

T.J. started counting off the reasons why it wasn't. "Her publisher's in New York, and I don't think authors actually go to their publisher's offices very often. Plus, I have to go to school during the week, and I really don't think my parents would let me fly to New York City on the weekend—just saying we could even afford it in the first place."

"So, we could hitchhike."

"There is *no* way you'll catch me hitchhiking *anywhere.*"

"Oh, pooh."

"And you're not listening. I could never get away from home for as long as it would take. I'm worried enough about getting downtown on my own—just saying we ever got her address."

"You worry too much," Elizabeth said.

T.J. shook her head. "No, you don't worry enough."

They fell silent then.

T.J. moved her mouse and clicked on her IM icon, but there were no messages from Julie.

"Well, what *are* we supposed to do then?" Elizabeth asked.

T.J. looked over at her. "I think we should try to find your parents, or some other Littles."

"Oh, right."

"I don't have a better idea."

But then providence provided one for them.

T.J. never read the newspaper, but they had an assignment for history where they had to take a current news story from the paper and show how it might be written up in a history book years from now.

It seemed like a stupid exercise to T.J. How were you supposed to know what would be important enough to make it into a history book? Especially this week, when there was nothing of major importance in the news. Or at least it seemed like that kind of week, since her father hadn't gone into one of his lectures of "what was the world coming to?" that no one listened to.

But she'd dutifully brought the paper to her room after her parents were done with it. She went and sat on the bed and started flipping through the pages, bored beyond words. She would have missed the notice, tucked away in the Arts & Entertainment section, if the rest of the paper hadn't been so completely and utterly mind-numbing.

But there it was.

"Look at this!" she cried, poking the paper with her finger.

She looked over at Elizabeth.

"She's going to be right here," she went on, "or near as."

"Who's going to be where?" Elizabeth asked.

"Sheri Piper. She's giving a reading at the Barnes and

Noble on Saturday morning. It'll just be for kids, I guess, but we could still go and try to see her." T.J. bounced on the edge of the bed. "Maybe we can catch her on her own before she goes into the store, or when she's leaving."

"Or if she goes to the bathroom."

T.J. pulled a face.

"What?" Elizabeth said. "People definitely do *that* on their own."

"I suppose. But the best thing is that Mom and Dad can't not let me go. It's on a Saturday morning—right nearby. They might even let me go by myself on my bike. It's not that far."

Elizabeth nodded. "This is good. Do we know what she looks like now?"

"I downloaded that picture of her from the Internet."

"Which was probably taken years ago."

"It doesn't matter. We'll know what she looks like when they introduce her and she starts her reading. This is so perfect."

So naturally everything went wrong.

It didn't start out that way.

It started out as good as they could have hoped. T.J.'s parents were fine with her biking over to the store by herself—"So long as you're very careful, young lady," her father put in—and even gave her the money to buy a copy of Piper's most recent book and a treat at the in-store café.

During the evenings, T.J. and Elizabeth worked on converting an old plush teddy bear of T.J.'s into an over-sized protective suit that Elizabeth could put on so that she wouldn't get banged around when she was in T.J.'s backpack. Or at least T.J. did the work, while Elizabeth directed, but the Little took equal credit when they'd finally finished the actual working version.

"Aren't you going to test it?" T.J. asked.

"If I have to."

"Isn't your getting inside the whole point of this?"

"That's easy for you to say. You don't have to do it."

"You don't, either," T.J. said. "You can just wait here and I'll tell you what happened when I get back home."

"No way."

It was easy to climb into, its seam held closed by Velcro once Elizabeth was inside. She couldn't really around move in it, but she was certainly protected from bumps and jolts. She had a limited range of vision through a hole in the bear's mouth, which also let in the air she needed to breathe.

"This is totally claustrophobic," Elizabeth said.

Her voice was muffled and hard to hear unless T.J. put her ear close to the teddy's mouth.

"But can you breathe okay?" T.J. asked.

"I suppose."

"I'm going to pick you up now and put you in my backpack."

"Just be careful."

"Like I'm carrying eggs."

"Uncooked eggs," Elizabeth said. "Not hard-boiled."

T.J. decided to ignore that.

"Here we go," she said.

She lifted the teddy bear and gently placed it in her backpack, which she zipped almost closed. Then she put it on and walked around the room a few times, before taking it off again and laying it on the bed. Elizabeth came out as soon as T.J. had unzipped it. Her unexpected appearance startled T.J., and she almost fell off the bed.

"Oh, for God's sake," Elizabeth said. "Who else were you expecting?"

"I wasn't expecting *anyone*. I thought I was supposed to reach in and get the teddy bear."

"I wanted to see if I could get out okay on my own."

T.J. nodded. "You just surprised me."

"Well, I hope you don't throw a fit when you're holding me on your lap at the bookstore."

T.J. stared at her for a long moment.

"What?" Elizabeth said.

"There's no way I'm holding a teddy bear on my lap. I'd look like a complete dork."

"How else am I going to see?"

"You don't need to see. You need to be quiet and not be noticed."

Elizabeth shook her head. "There's no way I'm staying cooped up in there."

"Then I'm not taking you."

They were still arguing about it the next morning—when they weren't arguing about what T.J. should wear to the reading. All week long, Elizabeth had been pushing for sexy with a little punk: short skirt, a tight top, and for God's sake, would she please wear some makeup? T.J. planned to wear her usual T-shirt, jeans, and sneakers, and now that Saturday morning was here, that's exactly what she had on. And anyway, even if she wanted to wear it—which she didn't—she didn't own a skirt that Elizabeth would consider short enough.

"You're not living in the country anymore," Elizabeth said. "When you go around looking like a hick, it's no wonder the cool kids don't talk to you."

"I don't want them to talk to me. I don't need to be friends with people who are going to expect me to be somebody I'm not."

"Well, no city kid's going to want to be friends with a hick."

T.J. wasn't sure how someone who'd lived her whole life like a mouse inside the walls, who was basically home-schooled and about as removed from the high-school social pool as was possible, could consider herself such an expert on being cool. But she *was* cool. She might make all her own clothes, sewing them by hand from scraps of cloth that she'd scavenged from T.J. wasn't sure where, but they didn't look homemade. And they were definitely fashion statements.

T.J. was torn. In some ways, she wanted to be just like those confident girls she saw striding through the school's halls or posing like models out in the schoolyard. But that felt like a betrayal—not only to who she was, but to Julie and Red and everything she had left behind on the farm. Because they'd had those girls at her old school, and she and Julie had made a solemn vow that, whatever else might happen in their lives, they would never become like that. They'd never let clothes and makeup and hairstyles become the most important things in their lives.

But Elizabeth was like the snake Eve met under the apple tree, endlessly whispering in her ear.

"I'm not saying that you have to devote your every waking moment to looking good," she argued. "But would a *little* sex and glam kill you?"

Probably not, T.J. thought. And it might even get her some interest from a boy, but she was torn about that as well. The boys here were so different from her old school. Everything was different here. Faster, edgier. It was hard to catch your breath sometimes. And it was hard feeling so unsure of herself and of what she wanted. It had never been like that back home.

"It's called hormones," Elizabeth said when T.J. broached the subject with her. "It happens to the best of us. Just stick to what you know in your heart is right, and you'll be okay."

"So why are you trying to change me?" T.J. asked. "Why do you want me to look like someone I'm not?"

"Because you don't *know* who you are yet. All you know is who you've been so far. Now's the time to stretch out and grow and try different things. To be yourself instead of just a junior partner in the family unit."

Yeah, that worked so well for you, T.J. thought, but she knew it was too mean a thing to say out loud. She also knew there was some truth to what Elizabeth was suggesting. T.J. just wasn't ready to take the plunge yet. She knew that people changed, that she would change. That one day she would wake up and look in the mirror and the T.J. she saw there would be a stranger. But she wasn't ready. It might be that she would never be ready. How did a person even know?

"I'm not the 'junior partner' of anything," she said. "And I'm going to the bookstore exactly the way I'm dressed."

"But—"

"And you're either staying in the backpack and behaving—"

"*Behaving?* I'm not some—"

"—or," T.J. broke in, her voice firm, "you're not coming at all. I can tell you what happened when I get back."

"Whatever happened to compromise?" Elizabeth asked.

"I don't know. Whatever happened to common sense?"

Elizabeth gave a large theatrical sigh—she was quite practiced with them—but T.J. only looked at her, her arms folded across her chest, until the Little finally agreed.

"Fine," Elizabeth said. "Stick me in a teddy bear. Stuff me into your backpack, which you'll probably shove under your chair and then the person sitting behind you will spend the whole time kicking his feet against it. Sip lovely drinks and munch on snacks while you listen to Piper read. Don't you worry about me."

"I won't," T.J. said, which so surprised Elizabeth that, for once, she had nothing to say. "So climb into your teddy-bear suit," T.J. added, "and let's get going."

T.J. talked a tough talk, but she still felt bad for the Little. She could imagine how claustrophobic it would be, stuck inside a teddy bear, inside a backpack. And then there was the worry of being banged around and getting sick from being swung about. But at least she could do something about that.

She was careful not to jostle her backpack too much when she put it on and walked down the hall to the kitchen.

"Are you all right?" her mother asked.

"I'm fine."

"You just seem to be walking so stiffly."

"I . . . I'm trying to improve my posture," T.J. improvised.

She was rather pleased with the line, since her mother was always after her about slouching.

"Well, have fun," her mother said.

"I will."

"And be careful."

"*Mom.*"

Her mother raised her eyebrows.

"I'll be careful," T.J. said.

"And you'll go down the block to the lights when you're crossing Crestview instead of crossing over at the end of Rosemary?"

"I said I would, didn't I?"

"And you won't talk to strangers? They still haven't caught that man who keeps bothering girls along the Strip."

"What about Ms. Piper?" T.J. asked. "She's a stranger, but I'd like to talk to her."

"Oh, you."

"I'm just kidding. I know better than to go off with some weird guy."

Her mother nodded and found a small smile that didn't hide her worry. "I know you do. I just wanted to remind you. It's my job to nag. And—"

"Better safe than sorry," T.J. finished for her.

"Exactly." Her mother kissed the top of her head. "I'll see you this afternoon. You have your cell phone?"

"Of course."

T.J. finally escaped into the garage. She wheeled her bike out onto the driveway, then shut the door behind her. Checking to make sure no one was watching, she twisted her head and spoke to her backpack.

"Are you okay in there?" she asked.

"Just fricking dandy," came the faint, muffled reply. "What do you think?"

T.J. smiled, got on her bike, and pedaled it out onto the street.

T.J. wasn't entirely unsympathetic to Elizabeth's crankiness. It wasn't just this undignified mode of travel. The Little was stuck in the house, day after day, staying inside the walls to keep away from Oscar when T.J. wasn't home. It had to be seriously boring, although she did have her TV. T.J. knew that not being able to go outside would drive *her* crazy. But there wasn't much she could do beyond what they were doing now: going to see if the author of *The Travelling Littles* could help.

It took her less than five minutes to get to Rosemary Avenue and then down that tree-lined street, freewheeling most of the way since it was pretty much all downhill. There was hardly any traffic when she reached the four lanes of Crestview Driveway, and she was tempted to cross over, but she dutifully cycled down to the traffic lights even though her mother would never know. When she finally crossed over and got to the bookstore, she chained up her bike with a row of others and went inside.

She was early and they were still setting up chairs for the reading, so she browsed the aisles for a while until she suddenly realized she could hear a muffled sound from her backpack. She gave a worried look around, relaxing a little when she saw that there was no one near.

"Just wait a sec," she whispered over her shoulder.

She hurried to the bathroom and, after making sure she had it to herself, went into one of the stalls. When she took off her backpack and opened it on her lap, Elizabeth's face poked out of the teddy bear.

"What's the matter?" T.J. asked.

"I have to pee," the Little said. Then she held up the doll's nursing bottle that they'd filled before leaving the house. "And I need more water."

"Well, no wonder you have to pee, if you drank all of that already."

"It's hot in here."

"Okay. So . . . um . . ."

T.J.'s voice trailed off. She'd never seen Elizabeth go to the bathroom. She'd never actually thought about it. She supposed that the Little had her own bathroom, or some version of one, behind the walls back home, and ducked in there when she had to go. But right now . . .

"What's the matter?" Elizabeth asked.

"Well, how do we . . . you know . . . do this?"

"You could help me keep my balance and I can just go in the toilet."

T.J. wasn't happy with the picture that put in her mind.

"I don't think so," she said.

"Well, I'm not going to try to balance by myself. It's too slippery. I'll probably fall in."

"Yes, but—"

"Fine. Just put me in the sink."

"What if someone comes in?"

"T.J.," Elizabeth said. "I really have to *go*."

"I don't know. It's just—"

"Then take me outside. There must be a field or something around here, right?"

T.J. nodded.

"So could we go?" Elizabeth asked.

She held out the doll's nursing bottle before T.J. could close the backpack.

"And don't forget to fill this," she added.

There was a field behind the bookstore, a little tract of wild land that lay between the rear access road and a commuter train line. Reaching the edge of the pavement, T.J. gave a quick look around before stepping in amongst the tall autumn weeds and shrubbery. She walked about halfway to the train tracks and took off her backpack. Setting it on the ground, she turned away to study the Dumpsters and recycling bins behind the bookstore while Elizabeth did her business.

"Okay, prudey," she heard Elizabeth say after a few moments. "You can turn around now—no bare bums to be seen, and I'm climbing back into my teddy-bear prison."

When Elizabeth was safely Velcroed inside the bear once more, T.J. zipped up her backpack and started back. Coming around the side of the building, she didn't pay any attention to the cluster of boys hanging around near the row of chained-up bicycles until one of them stepped in front of her, blocking her way.

They were all of a kind—scraggly-haired teenagers wearing a scruffy mix of skateboarder and heavy-metal gear.

"Excuse me," she said, and tried to step around the one who was in her way.

He moved with her, still blocking her.

"Excuse me," he repeated, making a mocking singsong of the words.

"Whatcha got in your pack?" another one of them asked.

They were all moving in on her, and T.J. started to get scared.

"Please, I don't want any trouble," she said.

The first boy repeated her words again in the same singsong voice.

T.J. didn't know where to turn. There were a lot of

them—seven, or eight—and they were all bigger than her.

"What's the matter?" a red-haired boy asked. "Don't you like us?"

"I just—"

Hands plucked at her backpack straps. She tried to brush them away, but then someone pushed her. And then they were all doing it, pushing her back and forth between them, grabbing at her chest, laughing and jeering. The backpack was pulled from her back.

"No!" she cried.

She tried to get it back, but the boy holding it side-stepped out of her reach. Then she tripped on the curb and fell, banging her knee. The boys all laughed. The one holding her backpack dangled it in front of her.

"Lose something?" he asked.

"Give that back!" T.J. said, trying not to sound like some stupid baby.

"Make me."

T.J. started to get up, but then a car squealed to a stop beside them. The boys scattered, taking her backpack with them. T.J. collapsed against the curb, her eyes filling with tears. Her knee hurt, but all she could think about was Elizabeth.

"Are you all right?" a voice asked.

She looked up to see a man in a blue windbreaker reaching a hand toward her. He was in his thirties, she guessed, with short dark hair and a long, narrow face without much of a chin.

She let him pull her to her feet, then had to let him

support her because her leg felt as though it wouldn't hold her. She didn't seem to be able to stop crying.

"Take it slow," the man said. "Catch your breath."

She nodded and did as he said, but it was hard with her pulse drumming so fast and everything hurting so much. All she seemed to be able to do was gulp air.

"Slower," the man said.

She nodded and tried again, a little more successfully this time. She wiped her eyes on the sleeve of her jacket, wishing she had something to blow her nose into.

"They . . . they took my pack. . . ."

The man looked in the direction of where the boys had run off.

"I swear they're like animals," he said.

"I really need to get it back," T.J. said.

She wasn't feeling quite so weak now and pulled away from the man, standing up on her own. His hands hovered near her in case she lost her balance again.

"I . . . I'm okay," she said, feeling anything but.

"If you're sure. I could run you by the hospital. . . ."

She shook her head. Looking around, she saw people just going about their business in the parking lot. If it hadn't been for this one Good Samaritan, who knows what would have happened to her?

"I just really, really need my pack. . . ."

"I'm afraid that's long gone now."

"But it's got my . . ."

Miniature six-inch-tall friend in it. Oh, Elizabeth . . .

"All my stuff's in there," she said.

The man gave her a considering look.

"I've seen those boys before," he said, "or maybe it's another gang of them—it's hard to tell, they all dress the same. But they often seem to be hanging around outside of Circuit City." He pointed to his car, still idling beside them. "I could run you over if you'd like, to see if we can find your bag."

"Oh, would you?"

Hope rose in T.J. Maybe they'd be in time to rescue Elizabeth. With the man at her side, surely the boys would have to give her pack back to her.

"Sure," the man said. He opened the passenger door. "Hop in."

But before T.J. could, she heard someone yelling from the front of the bookstore. She turned to see another teenage boy running toward them—except this one was neatly dressed and had a name tag pinned to his shirt. The man beside her suddenly grabbed her arm and tried to force her into the car. Reflexively, before she even realized what she was doing, she kicked him hard in the shin. He cried out, and his grip loosened enough for her to pull away.

She quickly backed up, sure he was going to come after her. But all he did was shoot an angry look in the boy's direction, then ran around to the driver's side of his car and got in. A moment later, it sped off, the passenger door still open and swinging wildly as he turned out onto Crestview.

T.J. stared after the car. Then someone touched her shoulder and she jumped. It was only the boy from the store. He had tousled brown hair that looked really good on him, and a kind face, but T.J. wasn't ready to trust anyone now.

"Are you okay?" he asked.

She'd just been swarmed.

Elizabeth was gone.

Some perv had just tried to kidnap her.

No! she wanted to yell at him, of course she wasn't okay.

But instead she burst into tears again and sank down to the curb. The position made her sore knee hurt, so she tried to shift, but that made her bang her knee. She started to lose her balance, but the boy caught her before she hit the pavement. He let go as soon as she had her balance and squatted in front of her. She couldn't seem to stop shaking.

"Stupid question," he said. "Of course you're not okay. Here."

T.J. blinked through her tears to see that he was offering her a crumpled-up tissue.

"It's clean," he said. "It just looks bad from having been in my pocket."

T.J. blew her nose in the tissue, then started to hand it back before she realized what she was doing.

"No, you can keep it," the boy said.

T.J. nodded. "Th—" She had to clear her throat. "Thanks."

The boy held out his hand.

"Why don't you come into the store and sit down for a moment," he said.

T.J. let him help her up, but she shook her head. Though her knee still hurt, her leg didn't feel like it was going to buckle under her. She was still shaky inside, but she wasn't going to let any of that stop her from what she knew she had to do.

"I can't," she said. "I need to get my backpack back."

"You're never going to find those guys," he told her.

T.J. thought of Elizabeth being jostled back and forth inside the pack with no idea what was going on. Then she imagined the boys finding the teddy bear, seeing the opening, tearing apart the Velcro, pulling her out. God knows what they'd do to her. Maybe pull off her arms and legs like she was some kind of bug.

"I really need to go," she said, and started off in the direction the boys had gone.

The store clerk caught her arm. "If you go after them, you're just going to get hurt worse."

"You don't understand," T.J. said, pulling free. "I have to."

The boy shook his head. "It's only stuff. I know it sucks, but you can always get more stuff."

"No, I—"

"You're shook up. That's understandable. First you get swarmed, then that old pervert tries to drag you into his car. But you need to take a time-out and think this through."

T.J. looked at him for a long moment.

"How did you know he was a pervert?" she asked. "You knew before he even tried to grab me."

He shrugged. "I didn't exactly. But I was already coming out when I saw those guys pushing you around, and then he—I just didn't like the look of him. There's been this guy on the Strip—you must have heard of him. . . ."

T.J. nodded. "I guess it was him."

"I'd hate to think we had two of them." He frowned. "Man, I'm such a dope. I had the perfect chance to get his license-plate number, and it never occurred to me until now. But at least I know the make and color of his car."

This would never happen back home, T.J. thought. The farm would probably always be "home" to her. She'd never had gangs of mean kids attacking her or perverts trying to pick her up when she was still living there.

"God, I *hate* this city," she said.

"What?"

The boy gave her a confused look.

"It just sucks living here," she told him before she started off again.

"Wait—hey, what's your name, anyway?"

"T.J."

"I'm Geoff."

Whatever, T.J. thought.

"Wait, T.J.," he said as she started to turn away again. "You got a good look at that creep. You should give the cops a description."

She shook her head. "I've already told you. I need to get my pack back."

But this time, it occurred to her that she'd make much better time on two wheels. Geoff followed her to the bike rack and watched as she opened her combination lock and pulled the chain free.

"Okay," he said. "I can understand your not wanting to talk to the police. I mean, who needs that? But if you chase after those guys, you're just going to get hurt worse than you already have been. And for what? For some stuff that can just be replaced."

"You don't understand."

"Try me."

"It's not about stuff. It's . . . I just need to get it back, okay?"

Geoff glanced over at the front of the store, then turned back to her.

"Then I'm coming with you."

"I'm taking my bike."

He nodded at the rack. "Mine's there, too."

"What about your job?"

"I'll explain when I get back."

T.J. thought about how easily she'd been about to get in that perv's car.

"Why should I trust you?" she asked.

"I don't know. I just know that I can't stand by and let you get hurt again. I've got a sister your age. All I can think of is, what if this was happening to her?"

Every moment they stood here talking was taking Elizabeth farther away.

"I guess I can't stop you," T.J. said.

She got on her bike and started to pedal off in the direction the boys had taken, wincing at how it made her knee hurt. She looked in the little rearview mirror attached to her handlebars and saw Geoff taking the chain off of another bike, which must be his. A few moments later, he'd caught up to her and they had pedaled to the back of the store.

The Barnes & Noble was the last store on the Strip. The field where T.J. had taken Elizabeth to relieve herself continued north, swelling from where it had been confined by the stores and the commuter train line, into a large tract of weeds and scrub. It was dotted with little islands made up of mature trees growing out of the tumbles of rock that had been dumped there when this was still farmland. On the far side of it, T.J. knew, was another, newer subdivision.

Southward, a service lane ran the length of the buildings.

"I don't know which way to go," she said.

Geoff pointed to a path that ran into the field. "There are more places to hide out in there."

"I guess."

"They know that someone might have called the police. If the cops do come looking for them, it'll be in the parking lots around the stores."

That made sense.

T.J. got back on her bike and started down the path, standing on her pedals so that she didn't have to feel the rough bumps in the terrain. It also made it easier to pedal with her hurt knee, though it didn't help stop the pain much. She bounced along the rutted track, scanning the field on either side, but she missed what she was looking for.

"T.J.!" Geoff called from behind her.

She stopped and turned around to see him putting his

bike on its stand. It wobbled on the uneven ground until he found a place it remained steady.

"What is it?" she asked.

He went a few steps in amongst the milkweed and goldenrod and bent down. When he stood up, he had her backpack in his hand.

"Is this yours?" he asked.

T.J.'s pulse started to drum loudly again, only this time from excited relief.

"You found it!" she cried.

She wheeled her bike over to where Geoff waited for her and dropped it on the path in her hurry to join him.

"It's empty," he said, "but it looks like they just dumped your stuff out."

He pointed to where a scatter of her belongings lay among the weeds. She saw her notebook, her wallet, a shiny lipstick container, and then—yes! The teddy bear. She picked it up, but all her hopes drained away when she realized that the Velcro flap was open. Elizabeth was gone.

"Did you have any money?" Geoff asked, retrieving her wallet. "Because if you did, they took it."

But T.J. didn't care about the twenty or so dollars that the boys had stolen. She looked frantically around, dreading, but expecting, to see the small body of a broken Little.

"What's the matter?" Geoff asked.

"She's not here," T.J. replied before she knew what she was saying.

"She?"

T.J. looked at him and realized what she'd done.

"My, um"—oh, Elizabeth was going to hate her for saying this—"my pet."

"Your pet?"

T.J. nodded, but now she was stuck. What kind of animal rode around in a closed backpack? Then she remembered Lucy Campbell, another of her friends from before they'd moved, and her unusual little pet.

"She's kind of like a ferret," T.J. said.

He gave her an odd look at the "kind of," but all he asked was, "What's her name?"

"Elizabeth."

"And you just take her everywhere with you?"

"Well, she, um . . . loves riding around in my backpack."

Geoff nodded. "I think I heard somewhere that they like to find hidden little places, but I don't know a lot else about them. Do they answer to their name?"

"Sure," T.J. said, though she had no clue.

Did Lucy's ferret come when it was called? She couldn't remember. The only thing she knew for sure was that anyone—pet or person—had to still be alive if they were going to answer to their name.

She stared down at the teddy bear.

Oh, Elizabeth. This was maybe worse than having to give up Red.

Geoff turned away from her and started to call Elizabeth's name.

T.J. touched his arm.

"I think I need to do this on my own," she said.

"It's okay. I don't mind helping."

"No, it's not that. She's just shy. If she's still around here, I don't know if I can coax her out of the weeds if there's anybody around."

If she was even still alive. And if she wasn't, how could she begin to explain the tiny body of a dead Little?

She wanted to cry again, but she bit at her lip and made herself hold the tears back.

Geoff didn't appear to notice. He was looking off down the path to where it ran into the woods on this side of the subdivision.

"I'm just worried about those guys coming back," he said.

"I'll be okay. I can see a long way from here, and I've got my bike. If they do show up, I can take off before they get to me."

"Maybe I'll just wait for you back at the pavement," Geoff said.

That was a perfect solution, T.J. thought. She knew she needed to be alone to coax Elizabeth out of hiding—*if* she was still alive, oh, please let her be alive—but she'd feel safer knowing that there was someone looking out for her nearby. She'd felt so helpless when those boys were pushing her around, grabbing at her.

"That'd be really nice of you," she told Geoff.

"Like I said, I've got a sister."

T.J. waited until he was walking his bike back down the path before she knelt down on the ground near where she'd found the teddy bear. Or at least she tried to kneel. Her knee still hurt when she bent it too much, and she realized that she'd broken the skin because she could now see blood staining her jeans. She had to lower herself down with her leg held straight out and sit in the dirt.

"Elizabeth?" she called. "You can come out now."

Nothing.

"Elizabeth? Oh, please come out."

She studied the ground. If she was her uncle Lennie, she'd be able to see if the Little had left tracks. Tracks would mean that she was still alive and well enough to move around on her own, and the only reason she wasn't answering T.J.'s call was that she was too far away to hear it. But all T.J. could see was the dirt in between the weeds. Mixed up in it were bits of small dry leaves, minuscule pieces of dead vegetation, and a few coarse, tiny stones.

If there was a story there, she couldn't read it.

She considered moving deeper into the field but had no idea which way to go. She couldn't imagine that, in this short time, Elizabeth had managed to get out of the range of her voice.

That meant that either the boys had found her and taken her away with them, or she was unable to answer because she was too hurt.

Or dead.

Tears welled up in her eyes again. Oh, what she wouldn't give to hear the Little complaining about something or other once more, like criticizing her fashion statements— or at least her lack thereof.

She wiped her eyes against her sleeve and slowly got up to make a sweep of the area, calling out from time to time. She found more things from her backpack—a pen, a package of gum, a postcard from Julie—but there was no sign of the Little herself.

She looked toward the end of the path where Geoff was waiting. He waved when he saw she was looking, and she waved back before she returned to her search.

What was she going to do?

She couldn't just leave without finding Elizabeth, but if she was going to find the Little, wouldn't she have done so by now?

She widened the circle of her search, but there was nothing to find and no one responded.

Finally, she knew she had to give up. She would come back, but for now she needed to go home and put some ice on her knee.

"I'm going now," she said to the empty field. "But I'll come back. You probably can't hear me, Elizabeth, but I really will come back."

She walked her bicycle back down the path. Geoff gave her a sympathetic look as she approached.

"No luck?" he asked.

She gave a glum shake of her head. "I guess she got too scared and just took off."

"You can come back again tomorrow and try again," Geoff said.

"Yeah, except by then a cat or an owl or something might have killed her."

"I'm sure she'll be smart enough to hide herself away."

You don't know that, T.J. wanted to tell him. But he

was just trying to be nice. And Elizabeth was smart. Maybe she'd find a mouse burrow or something to hide in.

If she was still alive.

Oh, she couldn't go there, but already her eyes were welling with tears again.

Geoff gave her an awkward pat on the shoulder.

"I . . . I'm not usually all weepy like this," T.J. told him. "It's just . . ."

"Hard. I know. I had a guinea pig run off when I was little, and it just killed me."

"Did it ever come back?"

Geoff hesitated, then said, "Maybe that wasn't the best example I could have brought up."

"It didn't, did it?"

"No," he said, obviously reluctant. "The next-door neighbor's cat sort of killed it."

"Oh, God."

"But that doesn't mean that'll happen here."

"I know. It's just . . . everything's so big, and Elizabeth isn't used to being on her own and way out in the open like this."

That, at least, was totally true.

"We could try calling for her some more," he said.

T.J. shook her head. "No, I need to get home and put something on my knee. I think I banged it up worse than I thought, because it's really starting to hurt now."

"I'll come with you."

"You don't have to," T.J. told him.

But she was happy that he acted like he hadn't heard her and simply fell in beside her as she started home, the two of them walking their bikes.

"So, how did you know that guy was a pervert?" T.J. asked while they were waiting for the light to change at the corner of Crestview and Bendis.

Geoff shrugged. "Like I said, I didn't. Not really."

"But you called out before he tried to force me into the car."

"I just got this weird vibe," Geoff said. "It's funny, though. From all I've heard, he only comes around after dark, or in some more secluded place than the parking lot of the bookstore in the middle of the day."

"I wonder why he would take the chance today like he did."

Geoff shrugged again. "Who knows? Opportunity knocked, I suppose. And I guess he thought it was worth the risk. They always go for the pretty young girls."

T.J. gave him a surprised look.

He thought she was pretty? If that was so, then he was the only one who did—except for that creep in the parking lot, and she didn't even want to think about him. "You know I'm only fourteen, right?" she said. "Well, fifteen in a month."

He smiled. "And I'm seventeen. It's not like I'm that much older than you. My dad's five years older than my mom."

Was he hitting on her?

"They met when she was still in high school."

God, he was totally hitting on her. Now what was she supposed to do? Here was the first guy—a nice-looking, older guy—to actually be interested in her, and she didn't have a clue what to do or say next.

She wished Julie were here. She wished there was some magic way that Julie could be seeing all of this, and then whisper what to do next—in her ear, like through some kind of secret spy device, so that only she could hear.

Julie would know—just as T.J. knew she herself would, if this were happening to Julie. It was always so much easier when it was someone else.

But Julie wasn't here.

Elizabeth would know, too.

But Elizabeth was gone.

"So, do you have a girlfriend?" T.J. found herself asking, and instantly wished she could take the words back.

It was a stupid thing to say, and now he'd think she was interested in him. Well, she was, but she had to find Elizabeth. Who he thought was a ferret. Great. She'd already lied to him.

"I have friends who are girls," he replied, "but not an official girlfriend."

"Oh."

"How about you?"

"I do, but I had to leave her back with everything else when we moved to the city."

He raised his eyebrows and smiled, and T.J. felt her face go hot.

"I mean she's my best friend," she said quickly, "but you

weren't asking that, were you? You wanted to know if I have a boyfriend."

Oh, God, she was such a complete dufus today.

He nodded. "So, do you?"

"No. Not really. I . . ."

The only boyfriend she'd had so far—not counting Hans Van Meer, who used to push her down in the playground in the second grade, and Jimmy Carnes, who took her to a couple of dances where he spent most of the time talking to his friends—was Tony Donatelli, and he was imaginary. She and Julie had gotten tired of the other girls at school always bragging about their boyfriends, so they'd made up their own.

The story was that they'd met the guys on holiday and kept up long-distance relationships that were frustrating, but fuel for many long conversations on trustworthiness, kissing techniques, and the poor taste that boys had in music and their endless video games.

Or so she and Julie said. She didn't know where Julie got her information, but T.J. picked up most of hers from Derek and his friends.

Looking back, it seemed so juvenile and pathetic. But that hadn't stopped her from sometimes forgetting and thinking that they'd actually had these boyfriends.

"Not really?" Geoff repeated, smiling.

"I mean, I don't," she said. "Not right now."

When he simply nodded, she couldn't tell if he was pleased or not.

"The light's changed," he said, and they walked their bikes across Crestview.

"I should probably go in by myself," T.J. said when they got to the end of her driveway.

She looked up at the house, but there was no one at the window to see their arrival. With any luck, she might be able to get to her room without being seen, though that didn't mean she could get out of telling what had happened. It just might go over better if she didn't look quite so disheveled, and if everyone could see she was completely okay before she had to start in on her story.

With any luck. Right. Considering how her luck was running these days, as soon as Mom found out about her being attacked, she'd never let T.J. out of the house again on her own.

"Are you sure?" Geoff asked. "I don't mind meeting your parents."

T.J. shook her head. "No, it's okay."

There was going to be enough of a fuss without having Geoff subjected to the third degree, as well. And then there was the matter of him maybe mentioning the ferret that didn't exist.

"Can I see you again?" Geoff asked. "Or call you or something?"

This was so weird. But T.J. nodded.

"Except, I lost my phone—remember?"

"Oh, right."

"But I'll give you my e-mail address. Do you have a pen and paper?"

He tapped his head with a finger. "Don't need them. I've got an excellent memory."

She told him her e-mail address and he rattled it back to her.

"You know what's a drag?" she said.

"Getting swarmed and losing your pet?"

"Well, all of that, of course. But I totally missed my chance to talk to Sheri Piper, which was the whole reason I went down to the Strip."

"That's right. We both did. I would have liked to have met her, too."

"Really?"

"Why are you so surprised?" he asked. "I love books. They're the main reason I work in a bookstore. And meeting the authors is one of the big perks of the job."

T.J. was curious about what kinds of books he loved, but knew she'd have to leave that for another conversation.

"I'll look forward to that," he told her when she said as much. "Maybe we can grab a coffee sometime."

"I'd like that," she said.

She watched him leave, gliding down the incline, until he turned the corner at the bottom of the street and was gone. Then she walked her bike into the garage and tried to slip quietly off to her room, but her mother and Derek were in the kitchen.

"T.J.," her mother said, "what *happened* to you?"

"I'm okay," she said. "I just got . . . swarmed outside the bookstore."

Her mother gave her a blank look, but Derek understood immediately.

"Would you recognize any of them if you saw them again?" he asked.

That was enough to clue her mother in.

"I guess. . . ." T.J. said. "Why?"

"Because I'll beat the crap out of them."

"You'll do no such thing!" Mom said.

But T.J. was looking at her brother as if he'd dropped in from another planet. Normally, if he wasn't ignoring her, he was finding some new way to torment her. So what was *this* all about?

Her mother closed the distance between them. She placed a hand on T.J.'s shoulder and brushed the hair back from her face.

"Were you hurt?" Her gaze went down to T.J.'s knee and found the bloodstain on her jeans. "Oh, dear God."

"I'm okay, really," T.J. said, though she felt anything but, with Elizabeth's fate still hanging in the air. "They just pushed me around a little and took my backpack, but I got it back. Geoff—this guy from the bookstore—helped me find it, and he walked me home."

Her mother's gaze went to the door leading to the garage.

"He went back to the store," T.J. said.

"But your knee," Mom said, returning her attention to T.J.

"It's just a scrape. But they took the money you gave me and my cell phone."

"We'll have to cancel it immediately. *And* we're calling the police."

"*Mom.*"

"This is serious."

Thank God she hadn't mentioned the perv, T.J. thought.

"I know it is," she said, "but what are they going to do?"

"She's right, Mom," Derek said. "They're not going to do anything. They're just going to fill out a report and file it away. It's not like it was back home."

T.J. gave her brother another surprised look. So she wasn't the only person in this family who still thought of the farm as home.

"You don't know that," Mom said.

"Sure, I do. Read the papers. Nothing ever gets done. They haven't even come close to catching that perv who's been after kids down on the Strip. What makes you think this'd be any different?"

T.J. ducked her head and let her hair fall across her face. The last thing she needed was for anyone to know about the perv, too—then she'd *never* be able to go looking for Elizabeth. Usually she couldn't get away with anything— whatever she was thinking was forever written across her face—but her mother was too preoccupied with Derek to notice.

"I suppose . . ." Mom was saying to Derek.

"Don't worry," he said. "The next time she has to go down there, I'll go with her. Though," he added, looking at T.J., "it wouldn't hurt you to get some friends to hang around with. Then this kind of thing wouldn't happen."

T.J. nodded. "But I know this Geoff guy now."

"He works in the bookstore, you said?" Mom asked.

T.J. gave another nod.

"How old is he?"

"Seventeen."

"Oh, I don't know," Mom said. "He seems a little old for you."

"*Mom.* He's just a guy. We're not dating or anything."

"Yeah, who'd want to date her?" Derek said with a laugh before leaving the kitchen.

At least that was more normal, T.J. thought. For a moment there, she'd been wondering if someone had replaced her brother with an alien pod person.

"We'll have to get you another phone," Mom said.

"I'm sorry. I'll help pay for it."

"It wasn't your fault, honey. I'm just glad you're safe."

Her mother fussed some more, so it took a while before T.J. could escape to her room. All she wanted was to have a shower, change into fresh clothes, and then plan how she'd go looking for Elizabeth again. Even though Geoff had been at the edge of the field, Elizabeth would have known he was there. She would have heard their conversation and just stayed hidden.

And maybe it had been better that way. If Elizabeth had shown herself, T.J. didn't know what she'd have done. Geoff would have wanted to see her missing ferret and she'd have had to lie some more.

Someone—probably Dad—had told her once that the problem with lying was that it never stopped at just telling one. Lies were like having a pregnant rabbit. One day you had one, but before you knew it, there were rabbits all over the place.

And lying just wasn't cool. If you couldn't live your life without lying, then maybe you should have a good look at your life to see what needed to be changed. Because while it seemed like everybody lied, no one liked a liar.

T.J. sure didn't. And she didn't want to be one herself.

And she'd liked Geoff—*not* just because he was the first guy to pay any attention to her since they'd moved from Tyson.

She was wondering if it was too early to check her e-mail when Derek stopped her in the hallway. He shot a look toward the kitchen, then put his arm around her shoulders and steered her into her bedroom.

"I was serious back there," he said. "About those guys, I mean. Point them out to me at school, or if you see them again. And then they're going to find out what happens when they mess with my sister."

"Derek, there were six or seven of them. . . ."

"So? I've got friends, too."

"I don't get it. You never seem to care—"

She broke off when he held up a hand to stop her.

"So you can be a little annoying," he said. "So what? That doesn't mean I'm not going to look out for you. You're my *sister*."

"I know, but—"

She broke off as he shook his head.

"No buts about it, T.J.," he said.

And then he surprised her for the third time by giving her a little hug before he left her room.

"You just be careful," he said. "It's not the same here as it was back home."

There it was again, Derek referring to Tyson as "home." But before she could talk to him about it, he had left her room.

She stared at the door as it closed behind him. What a strange day. She walked over to her bed, dropped her back-pack on the comforter, and sat down beside it.

She was still a little shaken. Her knee hurt and she needed to ice it, but that wasn't the real problem. What felt the worst was how helpless she'd been when those boys were pushing her around. She'd talked brave in the kitchen, and to Geoff earlier, but the truth was, now she really was a little nervous about going out by herself.

Those boys . . . that horrible pervert . . .

If she thought about it too much, everything started to feel strange and disconnected, as though her brain, her heart, her life was split right in two. One part of her was still the girl from the country, the one who felt as though it was only yesterday that they'd moved to the city. The memory and heartache of leaving was still so immediate. But to the rest of her, living on the farm felt as though it was a stranger's life. Not this one where creepy men tried to pull you into a car, or a gang of boys could just do whatever they wanted to you.

How could just a few hours change everything?

She kicked off her shoes, one by one, and fell back across the bed, too tired to get up and have a shower. Staring up at the ceiling, she felt totally alone, even with Derek in his room, one door down, and Mom in the kitchen.

It wasn't hard to guess why.

It was because there was no Elizabeth.

She blinked back the tears that threatened to fill her eyes. How was she ever going to find Elizabeth again?

She heard a bump against the door. After a second bump, the door opened enough to allow Oscar to come sauntering in. He made a circuit of the room, trying to spot the Little so that he could studiously ignore her the way he always did. When he couldn't find Elizabeth, he jumped up onto the bed and looked T.J. in the face as though to ask, Okay, where have you hidden her now?

"Everything's horrible," she told Oscar. "Horrible and wonderful at the same time."

She sat up and pulled Oscar onto her lap.

"I met this really nice guy," she told him, "so that's the good part, but everything else is pretty awful. And it hasn't even stopped being awful yet. You probably don't care, but I can't just leave Elizabeth out there on her own."

She lifted her head to look out the window.

"God, it's going to get dark soon, and *then* what's going to happen to her?"

She put Oscar on the bed, had a shower, and changed her clothes. While she waited for dinner, she took a pain-killer and sat on her bed with an ice pack on her knee.

There was only one thing she could do, she realized. She'd sit through dinner and Dad's reaction to this afternoon's misadventures, but as soon as they were in bed, she'd go back to the field behind the bookstore.

After dinner, the minutes dragged by as they only did when you had no choice but to wait for something. T.J. spent some time in the family room with her parents, watching a DVD that Dad had picked up on the way home. Derek was out with his friends, so he was spared. When Dad started in on the DVD's bonus features, T.J. pretended to be sleepy, thinking that if she went to bed, her parents might soon follow.

To kill time, she turned on her computer and checked her e-mail. There was the usual spam and a funny e-mail from her friend Trish in Australia. There was also one from Julie, talking about kids T.J. felt she hardly knew anymore. She and Julie had been drifting further and further apart ever since school had started, in no small part because T.J. had to keep the secret of Elizabeth from her. The two of them had never had secrets between them before, and it made T.J. feel weird and guilty.

She sighed as she reread the e-mail, trying to muster some excitement in the news from her old school, but without much luck. She decided to answer it tomorrow and clicked on the next one, which turned out to be from Geoff. Smiling, she sat up straighter in her chair.

Hey TJ. Hope things went okay at home. Got a bit of good news for you. Piper's doing another reading tomorrow

afternoon—this time at our downtown store. I can give
you a lift, if you don't mind riding down there in my dad's
old station wagon. Let me know. I'd need to pick you up
by 2 for us to get there in time.

Geoff

Okay. So it wasn't very personal, but he *had* asked her out
on a sort of date. Well, maybe "date" was stretching things,
but it was still good. And better yet, she could ask Sheri
Piper about Littles and Elizabeth. Piper might know how
to find her, for starters.

She clicked on "Reply" and started to type.

That is good news, Geoff. Thanks for thinking of me. I'll
have to ask my parents, and you'll have to come in to
meet them this time. I'm not grounded or anything, but
I can tell they'll be super paranoid about me going out
again even though I only told them about the guys that
were pushing me around. I thought I'd spare them the
perv. They're asleep right now so I'll have to wait until the
morning to ask them, but I hope to see you tomorrow.

She wondered if she should ask him not to mention her
"ferret," before deciding she'd deal with that tomorrow.
Then she spent a few moments trying to think of some
cute—maybe even a little sexy—way to sign off, but everything she came up with sounded dumb, so she just signed it
"TJ" and clicked "Send."

She really hoped her parents would let her go. And if

they didn't let her go with Geoff, then she was going to insist that one of them take her. It wasn't like she ever asked for much. She just knew she couldn't miss this chance to talk to Piper about the Littles and see if she could help her find Elizabeth.

Speaking of whom . . .

She opened her door and peeked out into the hall. There was no sound coming from the family room, and her parents' bedroom door was closed.

Was Derek home yet?

That didn't matter, she decided. It wasn't like he'd pop into her room to check on her when he got back from hanging with his bandmates. Although it did mean that Mom would be sleeping lightly, waiting to hear him come home.

She looked at the clock. It was almost eleven. Derek probably wouldn't be back until twelve thirty or one. She didn't want to wait that long, so she was just going to have to take a chance.

Leaving her door open, she went back into her room, put on her sneakers, and grabbed a sweater and jacket. She slipped out into the hall with the clothes bundled under her arm and tiptoed her way into the kitchen. Luckily, the hallway was carpeted and the kitchen floor was tiled, so the only tricky part was opening the door to the garage. Her luck continued to hold, and she was able to open the door, step into the garage, and close the door again without making any noise.

She stood in the dark for a few moments, putting on

her sweater and jacket while she waited to see if any alarm had been raised. So far so good. She got a flashlight from Dad's workbench, then opened the door that led into the backyard and wheeled her bicycle outside. When she closed that door, she waited again, listening.

Still nothing.

She walked her bicycle through the backyard and then along their property line to the street. She didn't get on the bike until she was on the pavement, and then she pedaled away, her hair blowing behind her as she got her speed up. There was a twinge of pain in her knee, but nothing she couldn't handle. She'd had way worse scrapes back home from fooling around in the bush behind the farm, or in the barn.

She told herself that if she didn't focus on it, it would just go away. And it wasn't hard to focus on something else, because it was very cool biking through the silent streets of her neighborhood. Everything was so dark and quiet. She'd snuck out into the backyard a whole bunch of times since they'd moved here, just to enjoy the night, but this was the first time she'd actually dared to leave their property.

It got tricky again when she reached Crestview and the border of the Strip. Here, there were still cars going by, and with her luck, some good-intentioned driver would want to know why a kid like her was out biking this late at night. So she waited a short distance back from the street until there was no traffic, then quickly crossed over where she was, feeling guilty for not going to the lights.

She had to laugh at herself. If she got caught, Mom was

going to be way more mad at her for sneaking out at night than for not crossing at the light.

On the far side of the street, she pedaled as fast as she could, through the parking lot, then alongside the bookstore, hoping that she wouldn't run into one of the security guards' cars. Or worse, maybe that perv was still cruising around. But she made it to the field without incident.

There was enough moonlight for her to see the path, though small details like a Little would remain hidden. That was why she'd brought the flashlight. She just hoped she'd be able to find the spot where the boys had dumped her backpack.

She laid her bike down in the weeds and started to walk carefully down the path that cut through the field.

She kept looking back at the bookstore, then over to the tree line, trying to judge where she was. When she thought she was close, she walked much more slowly, softly calling Elizabeth's name.

There was no response.

She might not even be in the right spot, T.J. thought. The field was big—too big for her to cover properly, looking for someone as small as Elizabeth. If the Little didn't make herself known, there was no way T.J. would find her.

But what if she couldn't make herself known?

What if she was hurt? She might have broken a leg and couldn't get close enough to T.J. for her voice to be heard. Or she might be unconscious. Or she might be . . .

T.J. didn't want to think it, but there was no way of getting around it.

Or she might be dead.

T.J. had lived too long on a farm not to be aware of how fragile life was. Foxes or weasels got to the chickens. They'd lost one cat to a fisher, a kitten to an owl.

Oh, please don't be dead, she thought.

She was so involved in what she was doing that she never heard the approach of footsteps, didn't know there was anyone else there at all until a flashlight beam suddenly came on and shone in her face, blinding her.

She automatically turned on her own, aiming into the other person's face, her pulse quickening into an adrenaline-fueled beat.

It was one of the boys who'd attacked her and stole her backpack.

Don't Call Me Tetty

I'M TOTALLY HOT and bored, and rethinking this whole idea of tagging along with T.J. to the reading, when the trouble starts. And then it all happens in a rush, like a hundred things are taking place at the same time. Part of my confusion comes from being tossed around inside a teddy bear, inside a backpack—which pretty much sucks because it's all out of my control.

That's nothing new, of course. Being a Little in the world of the Bigs, everything's pretty much always out of my control whenever I'm anywhere around a Big. Which wouldn't be so bad, I suppose, except that Bigs are always trouble. You don't need to spend much time observing them to realize that the one thing they love to do the most is be mean. They're pretty democratic about it, since they'll be hurtful to anyone and anything, but they especially seem to gravitate to putting the screws to anyone smaller and weaker than themselves.

T.J.'s the only exception—at least that I've seen.

So I'm not surprised that some boys are hassling her and

pushing her around, but I sure wish she had the *cojones* to give as good as she gets. She should carry a knife like all Littles do. Stabbing a Big with my knife, it wouldn't be much more than a pinprick to them, but we keep them super sharp and you'd be surprised how much damage a Little can cause. Ever run your finger along the edge of a razor blade?

If T.J. carried a Big-sized, Little-sharp knife—the way I figure any sensible person should—and was willing to use it, those boys would learn to leave her alone pretty damn quick. But she doesn't have a knife, because Bigs are different from Littles. They believe they have all these laws and social boundaries to keep the worst of them in check. The problem is, villains and bullies just ignore that kind of thing. That's the way it's always been. You don't have to be a Little to see that. You just need to have a brain.

So instead of cutting them, T.J.'s being shoved back and forth, and I'm getting more than a little motion-sick from the way her backpack is bouncing around. I can't see what's going on, but I feel it when they pull the backpack away from her, because I experience this sudden, sickening swoop in the pit of my stomach as somebody swings the pack through the air.

The feeling doesn't go away, because then they run off, laughing and jeering. They take the backpack with them, swinging it around and around, tossing it back and forth to each other, and there's me hidden inside, trying desperately not to throw up on myself.

Oh, this is bad, this is bad, this is bad . . .

That's what Plinky Doore always says when trouble

shows up. He's this character in a Little nursery story. It's funny what you think of in a moment of crisis, isn't it? Here I am, just turning seventeen, and I'm quoting a storybook character like some little kid.

But I feel small and helpless like a little kid. Small and helpless and sick to my stomach. And—I'll admit it—more than a little scared. Because when the boys stop to go through the backpack and find me, I'm really going to know what bad means. I'm bug-sized, so far as they're concerned, and boys just naturally seem to want to stick pins in bugs. Or pull off their legs. Or squish them between their fingers.

But there's no way for me to escape, and right now, it's all I can do to stop from throwing up. As it is, I keep tasting puke-Slurpees.

Those boys run for what feels like forever. When they finally stop and drop the backpack on the ground, I'm lightheaded and disoriented with that horrible sick feeling crawling up my stomach.

But at least we're not moving.

I don't get a chance to catch my breath.

They open the backpack and my hiding place is the first thing they pull out.

"Aw," one of them says. "Baby doll brought her teddy bear."

I have to fight off another rush of vertigo as the bear is tossed around. Then I guess it hits the ground because there's this huge jolt of an impact that I feel through every inch of my muscle and bones—even cushioned as I am by the soft plush of the toy. I think I black out, though it can't be for long. And at least I'm no longer in motion, so the bear must have been tossed aside.

"Here's her phone," someone says. "Hey, Ron. Do you know anybody in Japan we can call?"

"C'mon, Ricky," another one of them says. "We shouldn't be doing this. Just leave the stuff alone."

"Why? Is she your girlfriend or something?"

"No, it's just—"

"Relax, Vega," Ricky says. "Take this as a lesson on how to live in the fast lane: the strong survive and the weak lose out. That's the way it goes. So all you need to ask yourself is, do you want to be a winner, or do you want to be a loser gardener's son all your life?"

"He's a landscaper."

"Whatever."

"And no matter what I become," Vega says, "I'll always be my father's son."

"Yeah, well, that's your problem, isn't it?"

"Hey!" another voice says. "There's twenty-three bucks in her wallet."

"Score!"

"Guys!" Vega says.

"Oh, lighten up, Vega. You're turning into a complete pussy, and it's starting to bore me."

"It's just not right."

"Neither's bribery or corruption, but they happen all the same."

Laughter rises up at that.

"No, I'm serious," Vega says. "She was just a kid."

"A rich kid."

"We don't know that."

I know I should be trying to sneak off right now. Just pop the Velcro tabs and crawl out of my teddy-bear suit and make my getaway. But I don't know if I'm lying in plain sight of the boys, or where I am. And anyway, I'm too shaken to do much more than lie here and pray no one will think to have a closer look at the teddy bear and realize something's hidden inside.

"But see, that's the thing," Ricky says. "It doesn't matter if she's rich or poor. We have her crap and she doesn't, so we can do whatever the hell we want with it."

"Just give me the phone," Vega tells him.

"Hell, why not? Papá sure isn't going to buy you one."

"Let's get out of here," someone else says to a general chorus of agreement.

"Might as well," Ricky says. "Vega's sucked all the fun out of this place. I say we party at Eric's house. Your parents still out of town?"

"Yeah, but my sister'll be home."

"That's okay. I like your sister."

"Jesus, don't make me puke."

The voices are receding, and I let myself hope again. I might still get out of this alive. Of course then one of those creeps gives the teddy a kick. The jolt of impact knocks my teeth together. I'm airborne for a moment—not long enough to get sick, but long enough to make the landing hard, and I guess I black out again.

Again, it's not for long. I listen, but I can't hear anything, so I work the Velcro tab free and squeeze out of the teddy's stomach. I peer cautiously around me, but it seems I'm alone.

I'm a bit woozy and have to lean against the bear. I could just curl up on top of it and go to sleep for a week, but I know I can't stay. The boys might be back. Someone else might show up. I'm in the open, and whatever else I know or think about my people, I know that's never safe.

I take a couple of steadying breaths, then push back into the teddy just long enough to grab the water bottle and the bag with my hook and rope. Then I take off into the long grass and weeds, heading east, where I can just see the tips of a line of maples and birch marking a tree line.

My head clears as I jog along. My first priority is to find shelter. I don't know where I am—somewhere close to the bookstore, I'm guessing—but being out in the open like this is giving me a serious case of the heebie-jeebies. All I need right now is for some hawk to spot me, or run into a cat out playing lion in the savannah.

I find myself missing T.J. Sure, she's a bit of a Goody Two-shoes, but her heart's always in the right place. I admire her for that. More importantly—given my present situation—I was always safe with her. At least I was until those boys attacked her. But my being lost now and on my own has nothing to do with her. It was my own pigheadedness of insisting I had to come along to the bookstore.

I wonder what happened to her. I hope the boys didn't hurt her when they were pushing her around.

Oh, if I'd been a Big and seen that, those boys would've learned a lesson or two.

I look up to check my progress and see that I've almost reached the tree line. There are cedars here, too, which is good. Their rough bark and lower branches make it easy to climb to the safer branches higher up.

I'd slowed to a walk, but I quicken my pace now. Moments later, I'm in among the trees. I look back the way I came, but all I can see are the tall weeds and grass. Ahead, I see a chain-link fence. When I get to it, I squeeze through one of the lower links and then start looking for a place to hide for the night.

It's not dark yet, but dusk comes early at this time of year. I wish I had something warmer than this little jacket I'm wearing, because it'll get cold come nightfall. But that can't be helped. First I need to find a safe place.

The cedars appear the most promising. The branches are thick enough that they won't make easy access for hunting owls, and once I'm higher up, I'll be less of a target for cats or foxes, who, according to Little lore, tend to look for their prey at ground level. I can find myself a nook and tie myself in for the night. I'll be hungry, but I've been hungry before, and at least I've got a full water bottle. Maybe I can make myself a nest of leaves to keep warm once the temperature drops.

The wind is blowing away from me, out into the field, which is not good. It means my scent is broadcasting out there for anyone with a hunter's nose to detect. I cock my head. I think I hear a voice calling something, but it's out in the field and too far away.

I turn away and study my choices again.

Which tree?

I've my mind half made up on a particularly gnarly cedar when I hear—no, it's too quiet to actually hear. I *sense* something behind me.

I turn around slowly, and for one long, horrible moment, my heart stops beating in my chest.

There's a cat crouched low to the ground, motionless except for a twitch at the tip of its tail. Its dark gaze is fixed steadily on me, and I know that whatever luck I might have had since those boys attacked T.J. has just run out.

I don't move, because the one thing I've had drilled into me is that motion attracts them. But I don't have any other options. It's just too large. If you want some perspective, it's like a Big being stalked by a cat the size of a bus.

So this is it.

I edge my hand slowly to the back of my belt, reaching for my knife.

I'm not brave. My legs are shaking so badly I can hardly stand, and I can't seem to breathe. But I'll be damned if I'll go down without hurting it as best I can. With luck, I can take out an eye before it crushes me, but I don't have any hope that it'll be anything more than a last act of defiance.

I don't know how long we would have been there like that—the cat about to pounce, me with my tiny knife in my hand—but then a man's voice speaks softly from behind me. A *Little*-sized man's voice.

"You're doing good so far. Now I need you to move back to my voice. Go slower than slow."

I have no idea who the voice belongs to. The cat's ears twitch, but its gaze never leaves me.

"Come on, you can do this," the voice says.

I swallow, my mouth dry.

You don't know me, I think, so how do you know what I can or can't do?

Except for some reason, his assurance *does* give me the confidence to take a first slow and nervous step backward.

The cat doesn't like it. Ears flat, it crouches even closer to the ground than it already was, muscles bunching as it gets ready to spring.

"That's it," the mysterious Little says from behind me. "Nice and slow."

I can't do this, I think. But I take a second step—feeling behind me with my foot before I do the actual follow-through—then another. I know the cat's *so* ready to pounce. My fingers are tight around the handle of my knife, enough that they're starting to cramp.

"Just a few more steps," the man says.

In the meantime, so slowly that it's almost impossible to see it move, the cat has come closer. Belly to the ground, slitted gaze fixed on me. The tip of the tail twitching again.

Oh God, oh God, oh God, the Plinky Doore voice says in my head.

I shuffle one more step, then another.

I feel as though I have a telepathic connection to the cat. I can feel the tightness of its muscles. I *know* it's going to make its leap.

Then I feel a hand on my shoulder. It's there only long enough to push me to the side, and the Little who's been talking to me steps in front of me. It happens so fast that it takes both me and the cat by surprise.

Then before the cat can leap, the stranger lifts his hand. From where I've fallen I see that he's holding a whip. He snaps it right in front of the cat's nose with a sharp crack, and the cat jumps back as though stung. The man moves forward and snaps it again, close to the eye. A third time, and I'm sure it takes off a whisker this time.

But wonder of wonders, the cat turns tail and runs off.

The man stands watching the weeds into which it's disappeared, whip dangling on the ground now. When he finally turns around, I've got some of my breath back but don't quite trust my legs to hold me, so I just sit there in the dirt, looking up at him as he walks over to me.

He gives me a hand up, then turns to check for the cat again. I pick up my knife from where I dropped it. Wiping the dirt from the blade, I put it back into the sheath at the small of my back, then pick up my bag.

"Wow," I say. "I guess you've done that before."

He shrugs. "Spend enough time in the wilds, and you learn a trick or two."

No kidding, I think.

I know what he is now. The jacket and trousers made of some kind of shrew or moleskin's the big giveaway.

"You're a feral, aren't you?" I say.

Most Littles hole up in houses or other buildings, living in family units—small enough not to be noticed by the owners of the structures, but large enough to give each other comfort and support. But there have always been those who took to the wild and refused to be bound by four walls. The ferals. Which is what I thought I was going to be until I realized I didn't have whatever it takes to live that kind of a life.

Two or three times a year, we've had one come by to stay with us for a few days, exchanging news and gossip from other families in return for a home-cooked meal and some company. My brother Tad and I have always been fascinated by them, and why wouldn't we be? We're kids, and the whole idea of a feral's free and wandering life always seems so terribly romantic.

But we hadn't seen any of them for over a year, and this one's a stranger to me.

"We prefer the term 'ranger,'" he says.

I smile. "Yeah, and I'd like to be six feet tall instead of six inches, but what can you do?"

He turns to look at me, a smile twitching in the corner of his mouth.

He's about my dad's age—late forties—but his face is weathered and creased, his long hair pulled back in a ponytail.

"I never heard of a Little facing down a cat before," I say.

"We were lucky. She was a domestic—you saw her collar, right? So she has the instincts, but hunting a Little's no more than a game to her. A wild cat would have snapped your neck before you ever knew it was there."

I shiver at the thought.

He cocks his head and looks me over.

"You'll be Tetty Wood," he says. "I was told to keep an eye out for you."

I don't need to guess by whom. My parents must have run into him when they were finding a new house.

"Don't call me Tetty," I say.

"But it's your name."

"No, my name's Elizabeth."

He nods. "One you chose for yourself."

"Do you have a problem with that?"

"No. It's just . . . Tetty is a good Little name."

"And I don't particularly want to be a good Little, following every rule like some stupid sheep."

"Sheep aren't actually stupid."

"You know what I mean."

"I do. It's why I'm a ranger, rather than one of you housey-folk."

I have to laugh at that. I thought "housey-folk" was only a term you heard in storybooks. But it perfectly describes my family and pretty much every other Little I've met, except for a few ferals and this strange man in his moleskin jacket and trousers.

"So what's your name?" I ask.

He smiles. "The one I was given, or the one I took for myself?"

Oh, enough with the enigmatic-stranger shtick, I think.

"The one you'll answer to," I say.

"You can call me Bakro."

I nod. "What happens now?" I ask. "Were you told to bring me back to my parents?"

"No one tells me what to do," Bakro says, his voice firm. "Especially not housey-folk."

"You just said you were told to keep an eye out for me."

He smiles. "But not what to do if I found you. What do you want to do?"

"Go back to T.J.'s house. She's going to be worried sick about me."

"And she is . . . ?"

"My friend. She's also a Big."

Bakro's eyebrows go up, but he doesn't comment except to ask, "And where does she live?"

"I . . ." I start, but my voice immediately trails off.

How useless can a person be?

"I have no idea," I admit.

I tell him how I ended up here in the middle of nowhere, almost-dinner for a cat.

"And this T.J.," Bakro asks, "she lives in the house where you used to live with your parents?"

I nod.

"Well, I know where that is," he says. "But we'll have to wait for nightfall before we can leave." He thinks for a moment, mapping the journey in his head, I suppose, because he adds, "It'll probably take us a couple of nights."

That's so weird. It was such a short trip on T.J.'s bike, but it'll take us hours and hours to cover the same distance by foot.

"You didn't seem surprised when I told you that I have a Big for a friend," I say.

"You wouldn't be the first."

"*Really?*"

"Where do you think all the Big stories about little people come from?"

"I never thought about it," I say.

He looks over to the field where the cat vanished.

"We should get out of view until the sun sets," he says. "You're lucky. I happened to be nearby, cleaning out a new burrow for a hidey-hole, and came up for a breath of air just in time to see your trouble."

I'm embarrassed. "I didn't say thank you yet, did I?"

He waves a hand. "Don't think about it."

"Are you kidding? You just saved my life."

"We were lucky—that's all. And let's not press that luck. But it's funny . . ."

His voice trails off, and I wait for him to go on. After a few moments I start to ask him what's funny, but before I can, he puts his fingers to his lips and gives a sharp whistle. Once, twice, a third time.

"Don't be nervous now," he says.

"Nervous about what?"

But then I hear it, something coming toward us through the field. Not from where the cat disappeared, but from along the tree line. Something big running through the weeds. Something big and *fast*.

Oh, God, now what? I think, reaching for my knife.

Then I see it—a small dog. Small to a Big, that is, and

not even as big as the cat that almost had me for a snack, but it's still larger than anything I care to meet out in the open like this. Because dogs are just as much a danger to a Little as any cat or fox. Now maybe I'd be two bites to this pint-sized mutt, instead of just one, but dead's dead.

Bakro puts his hand on my arm as I get my knife out.

"Don't worry," he says. "Rosie's a friend."

A *friend?*

The dog bounces into our little clearing. Dancing around, she gives a couple of excited yips, then lies down on the ground with her face close to Bakro, paws stretched out on either side of him.

I don't know much about dogs except from what I've seen on TV. Nobody's ever had one in any of the houses where we've lived. This one looks like a cross between a Jack Russell terrier and a Chihuahua—and had to have been the runt of the litter to boot. But she still seems huge to me.

Bakro scratches her nose. "Where were you when the nasty cat came to eat us?" he asks her.

"You've got a dog?" I say.

My voice makes Rosie lift her head. I guess she was so excited to see Bakro that she hadn't noticed me earlier. She growls until Bakro taps a finger against her nose to get her attention.

"No, no," he tells her. "Elizabeth is our friend."

The dog gets up and comes over to sniff me, and I can't help but start to shake. I've never been this close to any kind of big animal before. But she only sniffs me for what seems like forever, then gives me a lick that nearly knocks me off my feet.

"Eew!" I cry as I back away.

"Sorry," Bakro says, except he's grinning so much I know he's anything but. "She's just trying to be friendly."

I wipe the dog slobber off my face with the sleeve of my jacket. That big a dog—relatively speaking—there's a *lot* of slobber.

Rosie settles down again close to where Bakro can reach up and scratch under her ear. She gives a satisfied sigh, her little tail wagging hard enough to stir up some dust.

"Come give her a pat," he says.

I sort of want to and don't at the same time, but I walk over and put out a hand and run it down her shoulder. The fur is coarse and stiff, not at all like that of the pet mouse I had for all of a couple of weeks or so.

"Where did you get her?" I ask, then I laugh. "God, I have *never* heard of a Little with a pet dog."

"Her previous owners used to leave her chained up in their yard," he says. "Day and night. They never let her in the house, and I never saw one of them walk her, or play with her, or give her any kind of affection."

"So you set her free?"

He nods. "But it wasn't as easy as that. For one thing, she wouldn't let me near her—not for the longest time. Whenever I came into her yard, she'd start up barking and growling, stretching out her chain as far as she could, trying to get to me."

"What did you do?"

"Well, you know. There are two things a Little does best: we're clever and we're patient. I went into that yard every night for two weeks, soft talking and bringing a present of kibbles. She'd have nothing to do with me at first, but finally it got to where she was at least quiet when I came into the yard and would eat the kibble. Then she let me pat her. I gave it another week before I cut her collar, and she's been with me ever since."

I grin. "It's like a storybook tale, isn't it? Like Jan Sproule and his red-tailed hawk."

"I suppose it is, except we haven't been off to rescue the chief's son the way Jan and his hawk did."

"Can you ride her like Jan did the hawk?" I ask.

My head fills with a vision of running wild and free through Big territories, the wind in my face as I ride, the dog running under me, fast and fast, and no one can catch us.

But Bakro shakes his head.

"No," he says. "Rosie doesn't like anything put on her—not a bridle, not even a collar so that she could pull a cart. She'd been chained up for too long, I think."

"Why would someone do a thing like that?" I ask as I stroke her rough fur.

Bakro shrugs. "Why do Bigs do most of the things they do?"

I think he's just being rhetorical until I realize he's waiting for an answer.

"Because they can," I tell him, the way my parents drilled it into my head over the years.

"Exactly. It's the one thing a Little can't ever forget."

I don't have to guess why he's telling me this. He might not have criticized me earlier, for claiming T.J. as a friend, but he wants me to remember to be careful around her, because no matter what there might be between us, she's still a Big. All she has to do is get mad at me once and she could just stick me in a jar. Or squash me without even having to think about it.

I'm not saying she would—because I sure don't think she ever would—but the point is that she *could*.

Bakro gives Rosie a last pat, then beckons to me.

"Come see this," he says.

He turns then and disappears into a thick stand of dried grass. I follow to find him waiting for me at the mouth of a rabbit burrow tucked in among the roots of the cedars. Rosie comes up behind me, but I'm not really nervous anymore and find I can just ignore her.

"Is this where you live?" I ask.

"Hardly. I just like to have bolt holes in case I get caught outside after dawn. I've got places like this all over. I sweep them out, lay in a supply of wood and candles—that sort of thing."

Right, except why would you want to even stay out overnight in a place like this? I decide not to go there and instead ask, "Isn't it more dangerous to be out at night?"

"Not if you want to avoid Bigs."

"I was thinking more of all the nasty critters," I say. "Like that cat that almost had me for a late-afternoon snack."

He shakes his head. "If you keep out of the open, you're mostly okay. And besides, I've got Rosie. She's usually much better at sticking around," he adds when he sees the unconvinced look on my face.

I'm remembering what it was like facing that cat. I don't see Rosie as much protection considering how that cat could have bitten me in two and been half finished with her snack before Rosie even showed up.

"But what about if you have to go out into the open?" I ask. "Crossing a street or a field?"

Because there will be a lot of them on the way to T.J.'s house.

Bakro smiles. "Then you have to be really, really careful. Now, are you coming in?"

I give the rabbit burrow a dubious look.

"It's fine," he tells me. "I've pretty much finished cleaning it up."

And it *is* fine, I discover, once I follow him inside. It's dark at first, but after we round a turn in the tunnel, the burrow widens out. There are candles at the end to light the way. The incline's not too steep. Bakro and I can walk upright, but it's a tighter fit for Rosie, who has to squeeze her way down.

The tunnel smells like the earth it's been dug from and isn't nearly as damp as I imagined it would be. Cedar roots poke through the roof, and I like this upside-down look at them. Roots grow pretty much just like branches, except you never really think about it because you don't normally have this view of them.

The burrow itself has dried grass strewn on the ground. There's a bed in the corner—no, wait. I guess it's what you'd call a pallet, just a grass mattress with twigs to constrain its shape. There's the firewood he mentioned, and a backpack. Rosie walks over to the bed and settles down beside it. She gives Bakro a long look, then lays her head down on her paws and closes her eyes.

"So, what do you think?" Bakro asks, obviously proud of the place.

"It's . . . interesting," I tell him. "Rustic."

He laughs. "I don't live here. It's just a hidey-hole."

"Right." I try to think of something to say and settle for, "So where's the fireplace?"

"It doesn't have one, as such. But there's a back way out—see here?"

He points out a smaller tunnel opening that I hadn't noticed the first time around. Because of the way the candles are casting their light, it's in the darkest corner.

"It has a good draft pulling out," he says, "so if I need to build a fire, I can do it there. There shouldn't be too much of a back draft."

"I guess you've thought of everything."

He shrugs. "Every ranger needs places like this in case they get caught away from their home base."

"What if some animal takes it over?"

"I'll block off the tunnels before we leave."

"Cool."

We sit on the pallet, and I stare down at my shoes, trying to think of something else to say. He doesn't seem to need conversation—if he did, I guess he wouldn't be a feral, living out here on his own—but the silence seems awkward to me.

"Don't you miss, you know, TV and stuff?" I ask.

He smiles. "Don't you miss the open sky and the sound of birdsong?"

"I don't know. I never really heard them. About all I know of the Big world is what I've overheard in the house or seen on TV. Mostly, I know what music's popular and what the cool fashions are."

"Fashion," he repeats. Not so much like he disapproves as that he doesn't know why anybody'd care about it.

"Sure, and let me tell you, it's pretty much a full-time job trying to figure out how to copy some of the cool clothes I see on TV, because I can only use things I've scavenged. That's what drives me crazy about T.J. She's a Big. She could walk into any store and just buy the coolest, sexiest stuff, but all she does is walk around in jeans and a T-shirt."

"Maybe she's more comfortable that way."

"I suppose. But it still seems like a huge waste to someone who doesn't have access the way she does. I sure wouldn't waste my time on jeans and T-shirts."

I can see he's totally not interested in this kind of girly stuff, so I let my motormouth run down. But then the quiet gets to me again. He and Rosie seem like they'd be perfectly content to just loll around forever, but I need motion, and if I can't move around, then I need to be talking. Or listening. I feel like there has to be *some* sound beyond Rosie's steady breathing.

I think it's got to do with being in such a confined place—such an *unfamiliar* confined place. I'm used to small spaces—I'm a Little, after all—but I'm also used to being able to move freely around. Restlessly, my mother would say, because I can never keep still for long. It's part of what was driving me so crazy, being cooped up in T.J.'s backpack.

But before I can find something to say, Bakro asks, "This woman at the bookstore . . . the writer. Why did you think she could help you?"

I shrug. "It was the only thing we could think of. I didn't know where to find any other Littles I could ask where my family might have gone, but I thought maybe she would know, considering her books." That makes me realize something. "But now I've met you, and you know where my parents are, right?"

"I know where they were a few weeks ago," he says. "But they were on the move when I ran into them, and they never said where they were going."

"But they were okay?"

He nods. "They seemed fine. And worried about you."

"I don't get what the big deal was," I say. "T.J. would never have talked about them. I've been living with her for weeks, and she never said one word about me to anyone—not even to her best friend, and I *know* that was bugging her."

"We're not all so trusting of Bigs."

"I didn't say I was trusting of Bigs," I tell him. "I'm only saying that I trust T.J. But of course that wouldn't make any difference to the 'rents or you, because what does a kid know, right?"

Bakro shakes his head. "Sometimes it's not so much a distrust of someone's judgment—regardless of their age.

There could be other reasons—good reasons, if we knew them."

"Like what?"

He hesitates for a moment, then asks, "Did your dad ever tell you about his brother Joji?"

"I didn't even know he had a brother."

Bakro nods. "Yes, that was from before he and your mother became housey-folk, so I can see why they might not talk about him."

"My parents were *ferals*?"

"Not exactly—"

"Oh, right. Excuse me. Rangers."

He shakes his head. "No, they were travellers—tinker-folk. They journeyed north and south, east and west, trading goods and mending what was broken in exchange for lodging and company."

All I can do is stare at him.

"Are you sure we're talking about the same people?" I ask. "Lazlo and Mala Wood, professional stick-in-the-muds extraordinaire?"

"That's a bit harsh," he says.

"Oh, come *on*. My parents are the definition of boring."

"Except perhaps what you viewed as boring, they thought of as a well-earned respite from an earlier life of hardship and travel."

"Say what?"

"Will you let me tell the story?"

I nod. "Sure. The one about the uncle I never knew I had."

He gives me a look.

"Okay. I'm shutting up. Except," I have to add, "I thought there were no more travellers. That there haven't been for years and years. There are only . . ." I start to say "ferals," but catch myself. "Rangers."

"There aren't many travellers," he tells me, "at least, not in these climes. The winters are hard here, making it more difficult to move unseen."

"I get it," I say. "And so it's from their glimpses of travellers that Bigs got their crazy ideas of fairies living in the woods and at the bottoms of their gardens."

Bakro shakes his head. "There is more to this world than any of us can imagine. Don't discount stories of fairies, or the First People who can walk in the shape of animals or humans, simply because you've never seen them."

"I just find it a little hard to believe."

"Says the Little, who—do I need to remind you?—is part of a people who are supposed to be the descendents of birds—"

"I know, I know," I say, breaking in. "Who lost their wings when they got too fat and lazy. And that's supposed to explain why our bones are so light and how we can get around in the land of the Bigs as easily as we do. Trust me, I've heard the lecture. I've even got the T-shirt. But *fairies*?"

"Why not?"

"And I suppose you've seen them."

He shrugs. "I've experienced things that I can't explain. And I've met people and beasts that were more than what they seem."

I shoot a glance at Rosie.

"Too bad she can't talk," I say. "Then we could explain how giving us a ride is just a friend helping a friend, not servitude."

"Or maybe," Bakro says, "she understands, and chooses not to help in such a way."

"But she owes you—for setting her free."

"No," he tells me. "I did what anyone would do—what anyone *should* do when they come upon injustice. She owes me nothing."

When he puts it like that, I feel more than a little guilty for saying what I did.

"You were going to tell me about my uncle," I say.

"Lazlo and Joji Wood—your father and uncle." He pauses for a moment, so I nod to show I get who he's talking about. "They were orphaned young and grew up a little wild. When their parents died, they were taken in by a great-aunt, you see—I think she was a Lovell, on their mother's side—but they didn't stay with her long. I suppose she was too strict for them. She was certainly bound to one place, with neither interest nor much respect for travellers or rangers."

"Which is what he became," I say, thinking of how tradition-bound my parents have always been.

"I suppose there's a certain measure of irony in that."

"Try living with it."

Bakro smiles. "No, thanks."

"So, what happened?" I ask. "What made him change?"

Bakro's smile fades. "The usual. Trauma. Unhappy circumstance. Your father was the bolder of the two—no risk was too great for Lazlo Wood in those days. You could have filled a storybook with all the trouble he got into. Joji was as bold as his brother, but not quite so reckless. They fell into the company of another Little named Rannie Catter and made a good living acquiring dollhouse furniture and fixings, which they traded to housey-folk."

"I still find this hard to believe."

Bakro gives me a look.

"I'm just saying," I tell him. "But go on."

"Thank you."

I lean back on my elbows on the bed and listen as he tells me the story.

~~~~~~

The three of them had a good business. Goods weren't made of plastics and such like in those days. You could still find furniture made of actual wood, and fashioned with a craftsman's eye and skill. Pots and pans weren't only decorative—they could actually be used. Today, you'll only find such items in museums and the hands of collectors who would notice a missing spoon. It's become harder and harder for a Little to get by—especially a new family setting up their first household.

Somewhere along the way, they made friends with a boy—a Big. Rannie was against it, but the Wood brothers couldn't resist, especially not your father, Lazlo, who, by all accounts, was the first to meet him. Suddenly, they had everything they could want—including safety. The boy provided them with every kind of food they might desire.

Cookies and cake, cooked meat, cheese, bread, and biscuits. It wasn't hard for him to sneak morsels from the kitchen that were a king's feast to three Littles.

The boy's father was a doctor, and his two older sisters had a half dozen dollhouses that had been relegated to the attic, so our three Littles had themselves mansions to live in. There were toys to play with. Think of it. They'd led a hard life, these three, skipping most of their childhoods by the need to survive. But now they had it all back again, with a Big for a playmate and protector.

But good as it was, it went bad, as things too often do.

Joji and the boy were playing table ball on his desk. In my day, we marked off goals and used a dried pea for the ball. But the boy had a real ball. He used only a finger to try to flick the ball between Joji's goalposts, while Joji used his feet to defend and attack.

No one's sure what happened. Either the boy flicked the ball too hard, or Joji was too close to the edge of the table—perhaps both. But over he went and broke his neck on the floor far below.

The two surviving Littles stared in horror, unable to move. The boy was horrified, too, but in his panic, he was all too able to move. Before Lazlo or Rannie could say a word, he'd plucked the dead Little from the floor and went running to his father's study, crying for help.

He meant well, no doubt, but it was too late for Joji, and the last thing anyone could want was for his body to fall into the hands of Bigs—especially not a doctor, with a doctor's astonished curiosity.

Oh, there was a to-do in the house that night.

Joji couldn't be saved. After studying the miniature man, the doctor placed him in a plastic bag and put him in the freezer to preserve the body tissues. And then he turned on his son, wanting to know where the little man had come from, how long had he known about him, were there more?

There was much shouting—and crying on the boy's part—until he was finally sent to his room with a stern warning from the doctor that they 'would get to the bottom of this in the morning, or he'd know the reason why.' Later, the surviving Littles heard him speaking to his wife about how his career would be made with this amazing find. He planned to bring the body to his office lab at the university and dissect it with full photographic documentation.

Lazlo understood only the half of what he heard, but one thing he knew: his brother was going to be laid to rest as a Little should be, in secret and with dignity. But how to get the body from the freezer? There are few places that can keep out a determined Little, but that freezer compartment with its heavy door, set high in an enormous appliance, was certainly one of them. Given time, they could have done it. But they didn't have time.

"We'll have to make the boy do it," Rannie said.

Lazlo nodded in grim agreement.

They waited until the household was asleep, then went into the boy's bedroom and put it to him. I'll give that Big this much: he took full responsibility for his foolishness. He knew how much trouble he would be in, come the morning, but nevertheless, he crept down into the kitchen, gently removed Joji's body from the freezer, and delivered it to the surviving Littles.

He never stopped apologizing, from when they left his bedroom until he let them out the back door. But Lazlo was too caught up in his grief to offer the boy comfort, and Rannie had been against it all in the first place. They took the body and disappeared into the backyard with not a word in response, or a look back.

They buried Joji in a safe place, and then Lazlo and Rannie went their separate ways.

I don't know what happened to the boy.

~~~~~~

He falls silent, and neither of us says anything for the longest time. I think about what he's told me. I guess it explains why my father's always been so neurotic about any contact with Bigs, but couldn't he have told us some of this? Couldn't he have taken the time to explain it to us and maybe fill us in on a bit of our family history? I still can't believe I had an uncle I never knew about.

"How do you know all of this?" I have to ask.

Bakro shrugs. "I got it from that same Rannie Catter who was once a friend to your father and late uncle. We travelled together for a couple of seasons, back in the day. He's the one who also told me that Lazlo later met and married the daughter of Luba Faher and had settled into the life of a housey-folk."

My grandmother Luba was another relative who didn't get spoken of at home. We knew her name, but that was about as much as either Tad or I had ever been told of her.

"Was she a traveller, too?" I ask.

Bakro nods. "The Fahers are an old travelling family. Your parents never spoke of her, either?"

"Just her name. They always made it sound as though something tragic had happened to her, and changed the subject whenever we asked about her."

"Something tragic did happen," Bakro says. "At least as far as your parents were concerned. She wouldn't settle down with them."

"So she's still alive?"

"Very much so—the last time I saw her—and I haven't heard different since."

"And now my parents are travellers again."

"Oh, I doubt it will come to that," Bakro says. "By now they'll have settled into some new house."

"Could you find them?"

"I could ask around," he says. "Someone will have seen where they've settled. But I thought you wanted to go to your friend's house."

"Not anymore. Oh, don't get all smug," I add when he grins. "It's not because of your story about the dangers of hanging around with Bigs."

"So you want to find your parents."

He so doesn't get what all this new knowledge means to me. Before, I was frustrated with my parents. Now I'm also mad at them for holding back this whole secret history of our family. I mean, it's no wonder that Tad and I always had the travelling itch—it was in our blood. And they totally should have told us about our uncle. Maybe then we would have understood their distrust of Bigs. Instead, they just fell back on "because we say so" whenever we asked.

"I suppose I'll want to find them at some point," I say, "but right now's still too soon."

Bakro strokes Rosie's back, but his gaze stays on me.

"What do you want to do then?" he asks.

"I want to talk to Sheri Piper."

"That author you told me about?"

I nod.

"Why do you want to talk to her?" he asks.

Unsaid is: Have you learned nothing? She's a Big, so she's automatically dangerous. But I ignore the hidden part of this conversation.

"At first I thought she might be able to help me find other Littles," I say. "But now . . ."

"Now what?" he asks when my voice trails off.

"Did you ever hear how some Littles are supposed to have learned how to change back into birds? Back and forth, apparently."

He smiles, and I know how it sounds. I got the idea from T.J., who got it from one of Piper's storybooks, so it's not exactly the most reliable of sources. But still. If Bakro's telling me to keep an open mind about fairies and shape-shifting spirits . . . then why not?

"You don't think it's possible?"

"There are always stories coming out of the city," he

says. "I've heard that one. I've also heard that there are Littles who have tamed rats and ride about on them like they were horses."

"This from the guy who told me to believe in fairies."

"I didn't say that. I only said you should keep an open mind."

"But you don't have to?"

He sighs, then gives a slow nod. "I think it's a ridiculous idea, but I'm willing to consider it. After all, we're supposed to be descended from birds. Why shouldn't we be able to change back?"

He says the words, but I can tell he doesn't believe them. He looks at me for a long moment.

"So you're going to go into the city," he says, "to find these flying Littles."

"That's about it."

"I can't help you with that."

"Can't, or won't?"

"I don't go into the city—it's too dangerous for a Little. There are few places to hide in all that concrete and steel, and the places that do still exist are overrun by cats and rats and the moon knows what else."

"I'm still going."

"I can take you to someone who might help you find a relatively safe passage, but I don't recommend it."

Bakro's someone turns out to be a woman named Mina, and he doesn't actually take me to her so much as to where

I could find her for myself. We spend the whole night hiking through fields and ditches until we finally come to this old farmhouse that stands alone among the strip malls and housing developments. It seems so out of place until you realize that it was actually here first and everything else got built up around it.

I've been nervous the whole trip, even with Rosie ranging around us, sniffing at everything a dog could possibly sniff at. But nothing drops out of the air to snatch us up. No cats or foxes show up.

Bakro leads me to what looks like a culvert in the ditch we've been hiking through.

"You go in here," he says. "Just follow it through to the end. You'll find a kind of door with a cord hanging beside it. Pull the rope and it'll ring a bell to let Mina know you're there."

I give the dark opening a dubious look.

"Don't worry," he tells me. "It's clean and dry, and it runs straight so that you won't get lost. And I've got a lantern here for you," he adds.

He swings his pack to the ground and starts to rummage around inside it.

"You're not coming?" I ask.

He shakes his head.

"But why not?"

"I'm not a city Little," he says after a long moment. "I don't have the mental stamina—always having to be on my guard, never a chance to relax. There's always someone awake in the city. There's always someone watching."

"But Littles still live there."

He nods. "And they always have. But we're different, city and country Littles. And . . ." He hesitates, then finally adds, "We don't much mix, one with the other."

"So all those stories about Littles turning into birds," I say. "They could be true, couldn't they? You just wouldn't know, because you don't talk to them and they don't talk to you."

"If such a thing were possible," he tells me, "then yes, they probably wouldn't bother to tell us."

That big a thing and they still wouldn't share the story of it with each other?

I just shake my head, but I don't rag him about it. What's the point? I guess everyone's got something they're stupidly stubborn about, and the one thing I know about stubborn people is that you can't change their minds.

So I just say, "Thanks. You know, for everything."

He gives me another nod.

"Good luck," he says.

Then he and Rosie head back up the ditch, and that's how I find myself alone in the tunnel that leads to Mina's house.

Like the rabbit hole, it's not nearly as bad as I imagined. Once I get a little distance from the entrance, it's dry, even cozy—though maybe too cozy, because the air starts to get a little close. The light from the lantern Bakro gave me picks out roots in the roof and sides of the tunnel and at one point I have to squeeze around a particularly large one, but soon enough I get to the end, where I find the little wooden door he told me about. Hanging beside it is the rope, just like Bakro said it would be.

I give it a pull and somewhere, far off, I think I hear a bell.

I stand there—patiently for me, I should add—and wait. But just when I go to give the rope another tug, I hear something moving around on the other side of the door. A bolt is undone and bright light streams into the tunnel.

"Welcome, welcome," a woman's voice says.

And that's how I meet Mina.

She's a tiny, shrunken woman—not quite a Big, since she's barely half T.J.'s size, but certainly not a Little. She uses a cane and walks with a pronounced stoop that makes a bow of her back, but even if she had been able to stand straight, she wouldn't stand more than four feet tall. Her eyes are large and round—Anime eyes, I think the first time I see her—and a startling bright blue. Her face is a road map of lines. I've never seen anybody so wrinkled. But she doesn't *seem* old, if you know what I mean. While she looks old, her spirit is anything but.

"So who told you about me?" she asks later, after we've introduced ourselves and settled in.

We're in her kitchen, which seems to be the biggest room in the house. It takes up most of the back of the building, with a big cast-iron stove for a centerpiece, old wooden cupboards, and drying herbs hanging everywhere. She's sitting at the table, which has had its legs cut down so that it's not looming over her. But it's still too big for me.

I'm on the table itself, sitting in a surprisingly comfortable wooden chair that she tells me she made herself.

I hesitate for a long moment, then finally say, "A guy named Bakro."

Mina smiles. "Oh, he's a funny man. He knows that I know that you Littles exist, but somehow he thinks that if he and I never meet, then it won't be true. Sometimes I really wonder where people get their ideas."

I nod to be polite. Actually, I think it's weird, too, but Bakro was nice to me, so I'm not going to sit around and dis him with a Big. Mina's not a big Big, but she's still a Big.

"I guess he's got his reasons," I say.

Mina nods. "I'm sure he does. But whatever they are, they're neither here nor there. What is it that *you* need, Elizabeth Wood?"

I tell her what I'd told Bakro, only a much-condensed version. She doesn't need to know about my parents or my botched attempt at going out on my own to live as a feral—excuse me, a *ranger*, ha ha. It doesn't matter what you call it, I was still crap at it.

"Hmm," Mina says when I'm done. "I wonder if you're any relation to the Woods of the Kaldewen Tribe."

"The who?"

"One of the city tribes of Littles. There's a tale that Jenky Wood struck a bargain with a Big for just such a thing— the freedom of wings. I didn't give it a lot of thought, except as a story to tell around the kitchen table, but then I don't have so much commerce with the city tribes of Littles. I think the Big in that story was a writer of books."

"So you think it's true?"

Mina smiles and shrugs. "Well, *I* haven't seen Littles turning into birds—or vice versa, for that matter—but I did once see a fox turn into a red-haired man right at the bottom of my field, so I won't say it's impossible, or even improbable."

"You really saw that?" I ask.

"Plain as I can see you sitting on my kitchen table."

I lean forward, elbows on my knees.

"Did he see you?" I ask. "Did you talk to him? What did he do?"

"I didn't get the chance to talk to him. He caught a bus and went into town."

"I'd love to have seen that."

Mina smiles. "Oh, he boarded a bus the same as anybody else."

"You know what I mean."

"I do. It was amazing. It's one of those memories that are better than gold, shining and wonderful every time you call it up."

"Can you introduce me to this Jenky Wood?" I ask her.

She shakes her head. "I don't ever see city Littles— they've no need for my help. It's you country folk that come ringing my bell."

I've never thought of myself as a country person, but I suppose, in her eyes, that's exactly what I am.

"So you can't help me, then," I say.

"I didn't say that. I can bring you to the Ratcatcher, and he should be able to help you out around the city. He might even know where to find some of the Woods—if not Jenky himself."

I look at her for a long moment.

"How come," I finally say, "it feels like everybody's just trying to pass me along to someone else?"

"That's just the way it works in the real world, Elizabeth. Out here, it's who you know that makes things happen. It's not like in those tiny close-knit households of you country Littles."

I feel like telling her that we're not all that close-knit—I ran off, didn't I? And besides, we're not totally isolated. A community can only exist on what a house can support, which is why we mostly live in family units. When our house was first built, a large family of Bigs lived in our house and we had three households of Littles, because there was enough for that many of us to get by on what we could scavenge. But those Bigs moved away and an older couple took over the house, so the Thomases and Bartels had to move, because my family had been the first to live there.

Then T.J. and her family came to own the place and it could probably have supported another household of Littles, but that was a moot point. The way things were now, it was open to any Little looking for a good home, though nobody would probably move in. I hadn't seen any signs, but I'm sure my parents had left some secret markings somewhere, with dire warnings of how the house had been compromised and so was unsafe for Littles.

But all I ask Mina is, "This Ratcatcher . . . he doesn't actually catch rats and, you know, ride them around. . . ."

"Like some rodeo cowboy?" Mina shakes her head and smiles. "Hardly—though I've heard the same stories as you have, no doubt, about rat-riding Littles. But the Ratcatcher's not a Little." She gets a pleased, teasing look on her face as she adds, "And he's not a Big, either."

I lean closer in my chair, thinking she sounds as though she's describing herself.

"Then what is he?" I ask.

"He's a gnome."

I guess my face goes all screwy with the astonishment I'm feeling, because Mina starts to laugh.

"Don't look so surprised," she says when she catches her breath. "Fairies are more common than most people realize."

"But . . ."

"But what?"

"They're not real."

"You could say the same about a Little."

"I suppose." I give her a considering look, then ask, "Is that what you are? A gnome?"

She laughs again.

"Oh, hardly," she says. "I'm only a very small Big who just happens to live in what most would call a fairy-tale world, what with the Littles and gnomes and all. But Littles and fairy did save my life. I was born a tiny, spindly thing—hairless, ugly, and red-faced—and my birth mother abandoned me to the garbage within minutes of my being born."

"That's awful."

"But true, and sadly, not as uncommon as it should be.

People are very good at throwing out what they don't want. Still, my story has a happy ending. I was found by a Little, and he went and fetched a fairy midwife, who took me in and raised me as her own. I never wanted for anything except human companionship, but as you can see, I'm not exactly what a man would find attractive."

"I wouldn't call that a happy ending," I say.

"It's all in how you look at it. No one's pierced me with a thousand porcupine quills. I'm not hanging above a fire on a goblin's spit, or locked in a box with only my head sticking out, or . . . well, any number of terrible things that could befall a body, if she wasn't careful."

None of which are things I've ever imagined happening to anyone.

"I suppose. . . ." is all I say.

"But you don't want to know about me," she says. "You want to know how to find the Ratcatcher."

That's not entirely true. I mean, I *do* want to hear about that. But I also want to hear about her life and fairies and all these wonderful and strange things that Mina's only hinted at so far. I suppose, being a Little, it's in my blood. That abandoned TV that Tad and I salvaged from the Bigs' garage and fixed up was a pretty new addition to our lives. Before that, we were like Littles everywhere: we'd always have time for a story—the longer, the better.

But sadly, although I appear to have stumbled upon a treasure trove of story, Mina's right. I shouldn't be trying to get them out of her. I need to find the Ratcatcher and hope he can lead me to these flying Littles. And for the first time, I actually believe it's possible. There really *could* be Littles out there who have learned how to change from Littles into birds and then back again.

"Just tell me he's going to be easy to find," I say.

Mina nods. "Today's Sunday, so he'll be at the Market. He's there every weekend."

"On Lee Street?"

The local news often has on-the-street broadcasts from the Lee Street Market, so I have a vague idea of what the place looks like.

"More like *under* Lee Street," Mina says. "This is the Goblin Market—but don't worry, you won't see many goblins there, and those that do come will be on their best behavior."

My face must look as blank as I'm feeling, because she adds, "Because of the Market-truce, you know."

Except I don't know. I feel like Plinky Doore trying to get directions from Tamalan, the hedgehog who can only talk backward and in riddles. I always knew the world was bigger than any Little could imagine, and stranger, too, in terms of the Bigs and their machines and their endless expansions of buildings and pavement and still more machines. But I never thought it would be strange like *this.*

"Oh, don't look so worried," Mina says. "It's not like I'm saying you have to steal a favor from the Queen of Gracie Street's bees."

I nod, no longer ready to admit that I have no idea what

she's talking about. Mostly, I find myself thinking that I should probably have just stayed with Bakro and let him take me back to T.J.'s house.

Mina takes me downtown by bus and then by subway, carting me around in a small wicker pet carrier, which is humiliating, I suppose, but I have to admit, much more comfortable than riding inside a teddy bear in T.J.'s backpack had been. Mind you, I'm not done with stuffed toys. I share the basket with a very lifelike Persian cat. It gives me a moment's pause when I first peer into the carrier.

"You know," I said as I stepped inside, "no one's going to think that thing's actually alive. I mean, it looks real and everything, but it totally doesn't move."

"Very true," Mina said. "But when people look at me, all they see is a diminutive, crazy old woman with a hunched back, so it's not exactly an added surprise to see me carrying around a pet carrier with a toy cat inside. Or would you rather ride in my pocket?"

"No, this is good."

And, like I said, comfortable. It probably would have been more comfortable if Mina hadn't insisted on chatting away to me on the bus, while we waited for the subway train to arrive, then on the train itself. But peeking through the holes in the wicker, I realize that she's right. People will glance at her, but mostly they just pretend she's not there. And truth is, I'm greedy for her stories. Who knows when, or even if, I'll get the chance to talk to her again?

She tells me how the house she lives in was the original

farmhouse for all the farmland around it—all those acres that are now taken up with housing developments and retail outlets. This last bit of the original property was owned, apparently, by a family of hobs and had been set up as a place of safety for fairies, Littles, and every sort of being that wasn't a human Big. The hobs didn't live there themselves. Instead, they had human intermediaries, and when the old man who'd last looked after it passed away, Mina's fairy midwife mother suggested she take it over.

Mina has lived there ever since.

"So when you were telling me about the man changing into a fox," I say, "really, that wasn't any big deal to you, was it?"

"Everybody's a big deal," she says. She pokes her head down so that she can look at me over the toy cat. "No matter how big or small."

"You know what I meant."

She nods, then sits up again.

"I do," she says. "But I never get tired of the magical beings I meet. Each one seems like a new surprise and wonder."

The train pulls into another station, and there's no more time for conversation because it turns out this is our stop. I brace myself as Mina lifts the carrier from the bench and disembarks.

There's a hike down Lee Street before Mina sets the carrier down at the mouth of an alleyway. She unhooks the door and swings it open. When I dare to stick my head out, she points to a tiny door set in the brick wall in front of us.

I'm not sure what it's made of, but it looks like brass. The word MARKET is embossed on the metal in fancy script.

"You'll find a set of stairs on the other side of that door," Mina says. "They'll take you right down into the thick of the Goblin Market."

I look back through the holes in the wicker, but people are just walking by, not paying any attention to Mina, crouched here in the mouth of an alleyway, talking to her stuffed toy cat. I suppose they won't pay any attention to me scurrying over to the door. Maybe they won't even see me—because a six-inch girl won't register on their reality meter. They'll see a rat, or a pigeon or something.

I look back at the door.

"Are they Little-sized stairs?" I ask, imagining the trek it'll mean for me to work my way down riser after riser of stairs made for Bigs.

Mina smiles. "They're fairy stairs—suitable for whatever size you are. Just as the door is a fairy door." She nods to the passersby. "Do you think they even see it?"

"I hadn't thought about it."

"Well, they can't. And *I* see a door suitable for a woman my size."

Here it is, I think. Real magic—up close and personal.

A shiver goes up my spine.

"The Ratcatcher's booth is easy to find," Mina says. "Just follow your nose to the best pastries you've ever smelled."

"He's a baker?"

"The best I've ever met, in fairy or human lands."

"So why do they call him the Ratcatcher?"

"You'll have to ask him that for yourself," she tells me. "Now I want you to take this."

She holds out a coin that looks like a penny. I don't try to take it from her. For one thing, it'll weigh me down too much. For another, what can you buy with a penny? I may not know much about the big wide world beyond the confines of my home, but I do know that a penny will get you nothing.

"Don't be obtuse," Mina says as though she knows exactly what I'm thinking. "This is a fairy coin. Just take it."

I hold out both hands to support its expected weight, but when she puts it in my palms, it's a Little-sized coin, supposing Littles ever minted coins. I stare down at it in wonder.

"That's in case you need to pay the Ratcatcher for his help," she says, "and it's only for the Ratcatcher. Use your common sense when—or even if—you think you should use it."

"Is it . . . is it worth a lot?"

She laughs. "It's worth what it needs to be worth, no more, no less."

"Because it's a fairy coin."

"Now you're beginning to understand."

"And it won't change into a leaf or dirt or something?"

Mina laughs again. "Oh, what an imagination you have. Now go on, or some Big with a bit more of the *sight* than most will notice the two of us talking, and who knows what trouble that might cause."

I start for the door, but then turn back.

"Thank you, Mina," I tell her. "For everything. I don't know how I can ever repay you."

"Do something for someone else in need," she says. "That's all the payment I ask for."

"I will."

"And one last thing: treat any fairies you meet with respect, no matter how strange they look, or how they might insult you."

That was just one more piece of advice to add to the rest she'd been sharing with me. The whole trip down, she'd passed along one bit or another, so many that no one could possibly hang on to them all.

But "I'll remember," is all I say.

I open the door and look inside to see a small stairwell going down and down and down. I hesitate on the threshold and look back at Mina. She gives me an encouraging nod, so I square my shoulders, close the door behind me, and start down the stairs, my bag on my shoulder, the fairy coin stowed away safely in my pocket.

It's a long way down. I start off counting steps but give up when I get to a hundred. The stairwell is well lit, but I can't spot a light source. Whatever it is, it would sure be handy when foraging between the walls of a house. I wonder if it's for sale in the market below. At this point, I'm ready to believe that I'll be able to find anything I want down there. I mean, it's magic, isn't it? And magic's real. Witness the little door that led me into here, the hidden lighting, the coin that Mina gave me—still safe in my pocket—that can change its size.

Of course, all I have is that coin—specifically meant for the Ratcatcher—so it's not like I can go on a shopping spree. But still . . .

After a while I start to hear something from the stairwell below. It gets louder as I continue down, but it's such a jumble I can't figure out what it is. Then I step out of the stairwell and I know.

It's the noise of the market. It's the hubbub of hundreds of voices and clatters and bangs and music and God knows what else, all spiraling up into a big untidy clutter of sound. But that sound is dwarfed by what I see.

Whoever built this place appears to have commandeered an abandoned subway station for their market, with various tiers of walkways, crowded with stalls and shoppers, tents and musicians and blankets laid out with goods on them. The tier that the stairs lets me out onto is for small folk, I guess, because if you were over three feet tall, you wouldn't even fit on it. I see odd little creatures barely half my size, some winged, some not, a few that appear to be Littles, except they're even smaller than me and I'm not a tall Little. There are others human in appearance, and then a whole lot of beings that I can't even describe. Some look like they're made of sticks and moss, some are part animal, or bird, or even insect.

It's beyond weird.

The tier below this one is for Big-sized beings, humans

and what I assume are elves, but so many more that aren't even remotely human. It's like some storybook spewed out its characters: dwarves and hobs, goblins and pixies, and I guess just fairies of every sort. Leaning down to look at them—at so *many* of them—makes me dizzy with wonder, except then I look farther down and every bit of me goes silent and still in disbelief.

The ground floor, where the subway rails would have been back when this was a working station, is for creatures so big I can only take them in from my vantage on this top tier. Ogres and trolls and giants. If I was down among them, I'd be no more than a bug.

Bigs are giants to a Little. These beings on the ground floor are too big for me to even process.

I look away from them to those more my own size, for all their many marvelous shapes and species. The light that lit the stairwell is bright here, though the source is no more apparent, and it's easy to see everything, though I have to admit I don't understand half of what I'm seeing.

Okay, there's stuff that makes sense. Vegetables and fruits, people selling various kinds of beverages, books, baked goods, clothing, incense, dried herbs, bunches of flowers, sparkling jewels that have to be glass—don't they?—bolts of cloth, and just all sorts of different kinds of junk, like clockwork bits and tangles of wires. The air is redolent with the scents of the food and drink, incense, and the smell of tobacco.

But then there are the things that I can't figure out. Little glass globes that look like air bubbles, except they're filled with liquid. Or the booth that has nothing in it but displays of what looks like dust.

What entrances me the most are all the little people and creatures flying about. The two upper tiers go right around the cavernous space, but many of the shoppers don't bother to walk around like I have to. Instead, they fly back and forth. Some of them are just wheeling and coasting for the fun of it.

The musicians—and like the shoppers and sellers, they're made up of every kind of being—are spaced so that their music doesn't bleed together. Or maybe it's some magic of the place that doesn't let the lute player near where I'm standing be overpowered by the obvious kick-ass music of the rock band a hundred yards away—and I say obvious because everybody near the band is rocking and jumping around.

I'm more than a little overwhelmed.

Just follow my nose, Mina said, but there are a thousand smells all around, and way more than one booth selling baked goods.

So I lean on the balustrade for a while, watching the flyers, until an old woman comes up beside me. She's got a sweet smile and kind eyes in that wrinkled face of hers. Her hair's tied back in a long white braid, and she's wearing a floor-length brocade dress that's full of tassels and gathered lace.

"Would you like some wings, dearie?" she says. "Auld Violet has nice wings for sale, all sizes, and her prices are fair."

Wings are what I'm hoping to find. Or rather, the ability

to change into a bird, then back into a Little. I think it's more than possible now. It's probable. All I have to do is connect with the Littles that know the trick of it.

But some of Mina's advice comes back to me, especially the fact that I'm supposed to be dealing with the Ratcatcher and no one else.

"I'm sorry," I tell the old lady. "Not today. And I don't have any money anyway."

"Pah. Who said anything about money? Auld Violet just likes to see people happy."

Not to mention talking about herself in the third person, but what she's saying wakes a little Mina-voice echo in my head.

Don't accept anything for free. There is no free in fairy. The costs are merely hidden.

"No, I couldn't," I say, and remembering to be polite, I add, "Generous though the offer is."

Auld Violet nods sagely. "Ah. Not one for charity, are you? Well, we can trade, dearie. Auld Violet loves to barter. A pair of wings for . . . oh, say, a lock of that pretty blue hair of yours. Too dear? Then a simple breath." She pulls out a bottle. "All you have to do is breathe into this."

And *don't*, I repeat *don't*, the Mina voice goes on, give anyone any part of yourself. Not a lock of hair, not a fingernail, not a gob of spit, nor even the smallest little dribble of pee.

I remember giggling and pulling a face when she said that, except she was totally serious.

Don't even give your word, Elizabeth, because a promise is like coin to fairies.

"Honestly," I tell Auld Violet, "I'm not in the market for anything. I'm just looking around."

She frowns and suddenly everything changes about her features. The cheerful eyes seem dark and mean now.

"What?" she says, with a dark promise in her voice. "Little Missy's too good for Auld Violet's wings? Someone else's business appeals to her more?"

"No, it's not that. It's just—"

"Take this as a warning. If Auld Violet catches Little Missy buying wings from another, Auld Violet will have her spleen in a pie for dinner, don't think she won't."

Don't let yourself be bullied, the Mina-voice reminds me. *No matter how fearsome something might be, Market-truce holds. Just be polite and go about your business.*

I clear my throat. "Yes, well, I'll certainly keep that in mind, and thank you so much for taking the time to talk to me."

Then before she can say anything else, I hurry off.

I cross some invisible boundary, and the sound of the lute is suddenly swallowed by the rock band. I dare a glance back, but Auld Violet has her sweet face back on and is chatting up something that looks like a stump, except it has legs and arms and a bird's nest for a head. I keep walking until I've left the rock music behind as well. I pass through an area with bagpipes, another where some little creature sits playing a kind of keyboard that emits discordant blipping sounds over a weird beat, and finally come to one with two young women playing fiddles.

And then I smell it.

Heavenly bread. Cookies that beg to be eaten. Scones that I know will just melt on the tongue. Pies that make my mouth water.

I couldn't not approach the stall, not even if my life depended on staying away. I stand there looking at one cake that's better than the pie beside it, except can it be as good as the scones dribbled with chocolate icing, or that plate of squares that smell like licorice and honey? Finally I tear my gaze away to look at the gnome running the stall. He's busy serving up slices and dozens of cookies and round loaves of bread that give off the aroma of nuts and oats, joking with customers, his hands always busy busy busy.

Follow your nose, Mina told me.

This can only be the Ratcatcher's stall.

He's sort of human looking, round-bellied and thin-limbed, but with just the right number of everything: one nose, one mouth, two eyes, no vines growing out of his shoulders, no horns on his brow. But on closer inspection, he's not really human. His face is the shape of an inverted triangle, the features too pronounced, and the ears that stick up out of his thatch of black hair have long pointed tips.

There's a momentary lull in his trade, and he glances at me. He looks me up and down and grins.

"Well, aren't you a picture of fashion," he says, obviously teasing.

I know exactly what he's talking about: it's this raggedy old coat I got from Bakro for the hike to Mina's house. I couldn't exactly wear the teddy bear like I had in T.J.'s backpack, so he'd given me this spare old quilted cotton coat. It had a bit of a smell of mothballs and looked awful, but I was toasty warm in it.

"It's better than no coat at all," I tell him.

"And isn't that the truth? What can I get for you?"

"Nothing. I'm just . . . excuse me, but are you the Ratcatcher?"

His brows lift. "I am indeed. And you are?"

"Elizabeth."

"A good name, that. A royal name."

I shrug. What are you supposed to say to that?

He looks me up and down once more.

"So who sent you to me?" he asks.

"Mina."

"And she told you I would help you?"

I shake my head. "She just told me to talk to you. That you might help me."

He smiles. "That's Mina. Very careful with her promises, that one. You look a little hungry—would you like a pie?"

I'd love a pie, except even though he's the one Mina sent me to see, I figure the "don't take anything for free" rule still holds. And buying myself a pie doesn't seem remotely close to a good enough reason to use the coin Mina gave me.

His smile widens as I continue to hesitate. "You've been listening to her warnings. That's good. Tell you what. Help me out in the stall and earn yourself a pie. We can talk about why you wanted to see me at the end of the day."

"I don't know anything about what you're selling, or what it costs."

Or what people are expected to pay for it. Locks of hair? A spit on the palm?

He tosses me an apron.

"Don't worry about that. You can fetch and bag the purchases."

I catch the apron automatically. Before I can say yes or no, a new wave of customers descends on the stall. He doesn't say anything, just lifts his eyebrows again, so I come into the stall. I take off my coat, stow it away under a counter with my bag, and put on the apron, which is big, but surprisingly not too big for me. Either his usual assistant is around my size, or it's more fairy magic.

Whatever. I don't even want to think about it anymore because it makes my head hurt when I do.

Instead, I just become a baker's apprentice for the afternoon.

"So how do you like your pie?" the Ratcatcher asks me at the end of the day.

I look up, suddenly embarrassed at my greediness, my lips and chin smeared with spicy apple filling. My hands, holding the uneaten two-thirds of the pie, are just as messy. After working all afternoon in the stall with the delicious smells constantly wafting up around me, as soon as the Ratcatcher told me to help myself, I snatched the pie and dug right in like some feral who hasn't eaten for days. Pathetic, I know, but you try spending an afternoon smelling and packaging but not tasting. It just about killed me.

"'S good," I manage with a full mouth.

He grins—amused at my indulgence, but pleased, too.

"You did well today," he says. "I've made the same offer to others, but they never pitched in with as good a spirit, nor were they as helpful. I only ever needed to show you how to do a thing once."

I swallow the bite that was filling my mouth and, with a little regret, hold off having another.

"It was kind of fun," I tell him.

"You have a knack for it—especially the way you treated my customers. They'll miss you next weekend." He pauses, then adds, "How's your baking?"

"Nothing like yours." Then I have to give him a curious look. "Are you offering me a job?"

"Would you take it if I was?"

It's nothing I'd ever considered, but when he puts it to me like that, I have a serious think about it, because I *did* have fun this afternoon, and considering the varied clientele, I couldn't see getting bored of it in a hurry. I didn't see any Littles, but pretty much every small-statured storybook character from a fairy tale seemed to come to the Ratcatcher's booth at one point or another this afternoon.

"Maybe," I say. "But first I have this thing I need to do."

"Ah, yes. The reason you came to me in the first place. What *did* bring you down to the Goblin Market, all on your own and in a borrowed coat?"

I'd found it important to let him know that the coat wasn't mine, who knows why. It's not like he's a fashion plate himself in his corduroy trousers, cotton shirt, and apron, all covered with a fine dusting of flour and spices, not to mention a varied collection of smears from various fruit and candied fillings. My own apron is almost as messy.

"It's kind of a long story," I say.

"Then start at the end, and we can work our way back if we need to."

That's hard for a Little, to tell a story the wrong way around, but I suppose I can do it. I look for somewhere to set down my half-eaten pie, and he hands me a napkin. I wrap it up and put it down on the counter where I'm sitting, right beside the mug of hot chocolate that he'd bought me from a nearby stall, which is probably the best I've ever tasted, bar none. I wipe my hands on my apron, adding to its sticky chaos.

"I'm trying to find another Little," I tell him. "His name's Jenky Wood, but any of his family will do."

He gets a funny, almost sad look when I say that.

"What?" I say.

"You're looking for wings."

"Sort of, I guess. More like the trick of changing back into a bird."

He nods. "Because it's in your blood, and once you learn that old forgotten word that she spoke, your blood will remember."

I give him a totally blank look. "Say what?"

"You're not the first Little to come looking for your lost heritage," he says. "And I certainly understand the impulse. From time to time, I've wanted wings myself—who hasn't? But the ones they sell here in the market are chancy things at best. Pretty, oh yes. They make sure of that. But too many of them fade away at the most inopportune of times, such as when you're a hundred feet in the air, soaring on the winds, and then, poof. Suddenly your wings are no more, and down you plummet."

I get a lurch in my stomach just thinking of it.

He leans closer, his features serious. "It's the same with this business with Littles and birds. It doesn't always take. And sometimes, it does take, only it doesn't go away. The Little is a bird forever. And sometimes it wears off, and if you're in flight at the time, well, the only thing between yourself and the ground will be the handfuls of air you're clutching as you try to slow yourself down." He cocks his head at the unhappy look on my face and adds, "You don't hear about that, do you, living out in the country the way you do? That's the part they don't tell you."

"No one's ever told us anything," I say. "I only ever thought Littles turning into birds was something out of a storybook until I met Mina."

He nods. "That's right. You don't get along, you country Littles and your city cousins."

"I guess. Seems to me like nobody really knows how to get along. Nobody's looking out for the other person."

"Well, I'm trying to," he says.

"Because you know what's best for me. Everybody knows what's best for me except me."

He shakes his head. "I'm just telling you it's dangerous, that's all. The choice is yours to make."

"So, you're not going to try to talk me out of it—I mean, any more than you already did?"

He gives me another shake of his head. "But just let me add one more thing—no matter how far you go with this, you can always step back. Even if you gain the ability to change, you don't have to actually do it unless *you* want to. Unless *you* feel safe about it."

"I guess. The thing I don't get is, why would it fail, if the change is in our blood?"

"I don't know. I'm a baker, not a deep thinker. But I have noticed this: the ones for whom it's most likely to fail are those who seem the most human in appearance."

I give him a blank look because I totally don't have any idea what he's talking about.

He smiles. "Have you not met other Littles who are more . . . birdlike than yourself? The ones with fat bird bodies and spindly limbs?" His smile widens. "Though they're good gnomish shapes, of course."

I think about that and realize it's true. Not in my family so much, but I've met other Littles who are just like he described.

"I guess I have," I say.

"It seems to me that their blood is closer to that old bird blood of yours, while Littles such as you are . . ." He thinks for a moment—looking for the right word, I realize, when he adds, "More evolved."

"So you think it'll fail for me."

"I didn't say exactly that. But from my observations, you'd be more prone to failure. However," he goes on before I can say anything, "that's not to say it wouldn't work for you. I've seen it stick for others just as human in appearance as you."

I give a slow nod. "Which puts me right back at square one in terms of making a decision, but knowing there's not the best of chances it'll work out the way I want."

"I'm sorry. I'd say that one should be content with what one is, so it's best to leave well enough alone, except you do have the bird blood in you."

"For all the apparent good it does me."

He doesn't say anything in response. But what's he supposed to say?

"I still have to talk to them," I tell him. "For my own peace of mind. Just to know."

"Of course you do."

I think back to what he said when we began talking about this.

"What did you mean about someone speaking some forgotten word?" I ask.

"Do they teach you nothing in your Little schools?" he says, smiling to show that he's teasing.

"We don't have schools—at least I've never been to one. Maybe it's different for city Littles."

He nods. "Maybe it is."

"So if I had gone to school, what would I have learned?"

"That language is the oldest of the magics," he tells me. "In the long ago, there was an old tribe of words sleeping unspoken in the darkness. In this land, they say it was Raven who woke those words as he stirred the world out of that old cauldron of his. Other places have different stories about how it all began. But the words were always there first, forgotten before they were even heard."

"How can something be forgotten if it was never known in the first place?"

"That's a good question," he says, "for which I have no answer. It's just the way the story's told."

"What happened to these words?" I ask.

"They remain forgotten. But a few faint echoes of them remain, and if one has the knowledge, if one has the craft and the will, they can be used to make changes in the fabric of What Is, because What Is only exists as it does because we've all agreed to its shape and meaning, using the words we do have to bind it into place. It's like the true name of a thing. If you know that name, it gives you power over it—doesn't matter if it's a stone or a tree or a being."

"I've heard of that," I say.

He nods. "So the story goes that Jenky Wood was sent by the leaders of his tribe to see a woman who had written stories about them, and she, in turn, asked for the help of an old spirit who knew enough of one of those forgotten words to give the gift of change back to Wood and his people."

"Her name's Sheri Piper," I say.

He cocks an eyebrow. "You *know* this spirit?"

"I meant, that's who the writer was. T.J. told me about her."

And then I have to explain who T.J. is, and how we got separated, and everything that brought me here into the middle of the city to talk to him.

"She's going to be so worried," I say as I finish up, "but dummy that I am, I don't even know her last name, or where she lives, so there's no way I can get in touch with her to let her know I'm okay."

"Perhaps I can help you with that," he says. "You say this Bakro knows where she lives?"

I nod. "But how would you ever find him?"

"Mina will tell me. She knows all the gossip north of the city. You Littles might think you wander about, stealthy and secret, but there are always eyes watching. Hobs and crows and squirrels and all."

"You can talk to animals?"

He smiles. "Not all animals are what they seem."

I remember Mina telling me about a fox that could change into a man.

"If you could get word to T.J., I'd be so grateful," I say.

He waves a hand to say it's nothing.

"Come," he says. "Let's finish tidying up here, and then we'll see if we can find your cousin Jenky."

"I don't know that he's my actual cousin."

"He's a Wood and you're a Wood—that seems close enough for me."

"I suppose. . . ."

We go back to bagging up the unsold buns and pies and breads and cakes, of which there aren't many. We wipe down the counters, sweep the floor of the stall, and generally get things ready for next weekend.

"Can I ask you something personal?" I say after a bit.

He leans on his broom to look at me. "Of course."

"Why are you called the Ratcatcher?"

"Because that's what I do best."

"But I thought you were a baker."

"I am," he says. "That's what I *like* to do best, but I was born a Stourn, and among my people, Stourns have always made the best ratcatchers. Hedley Stourn—that would be my speaking name, and you can feel free to use it."

"I'll use whatever you'd like me to."

"Then Hedley will do. Anyway," he goes on, "Monday to Thursday, I work the one trade, then Friday I bake, and here I am on the weekends."

"What's it like catching a rat?" I ask.

I've always been fascinated and repelled by them, but then there are two kinds of rats. There are the ones that haunt the nightmares of Littles—fierce, dark-eyed, and sleek. The kind of creature you *don't* want to meet when you're creeping across a rafter, or sneaking about in the narrow spaces between the walls. But then there are the storybook rats, like wise old Samuel Thatchett, the scholar that all the Woody Dell animals took their problems to, or tawny-eyed Rendilly, who helped Moira Strubben when she fell out of the painting she lived in and got lost in the real world.

"It's like anything else," he says. "It has its good and its bad moments."

"But rats are so fierce."

Hedley laughs. "I suppose they can be, especially to a Little, but the reason we Stourn gnomes are such good rat-catchers is that we can talk to them. 'Ratcatcher' is somewhat of a misnomer. What we really do is go to the places where they're causing a disruption and talk them into going somewhere else. There's rarely much fierceness involved, unless it's a fierce glare to make a point."

"You don't kill them?"

"Moon, no! Why would I do such a thing?"

I shrug. "I don't know. I thought that's what happened to vermin."

I'm thinking of the mice and bugs that are usually dealt with in such a final manner when they invade the home of a Big.

"I wouldn't go calling them that," Hedley says. "Rats are like everyone else. They have histories and language, families and tribes."

"I guess it's different when you're the size of a meal."

"You just need to find a commonality with them. Most anything will leave you alone if you can manage that."

"Even hawks and cats and owls?"

Hedley sighs. "Probably not. But that's only because it's in their nature to hunt. They can't live on bread and vegetables the way we can. They intend no cruelty by it."

"Oh, well, that's a relief!"

He laughs.

"Are you about done there?" he asks as he sweeps the last of the dirt from his side of the stall into a dustbin.

"I think so."

At least I'm done cleaning and tidying. But I've just remembered something else. I dig into my pocket and take out the coin Mina gave me. I hold it out to him.

"What do you have there?" Hedley asks.

"It's this magic coin that Mina gave me. I guess it was to pay you for helping me. She said that I'd know the right time to offer it up, but you know what? You've been so nice to me, letting me help you out in the stall and all, and not asking me for anything more than the little work I did, that I just want you to have it anyway."

"You say Mina gave it to you specifically to trade to me?"

I nod. He's still just looking at it.

"Is there something wrong with it?" I ask.

"Do you know where it comes from?"

"I just told you. Mina gave it to me."

"But before that," he says.

I shake my head. "She never said."

"It's from a wishing well." His nostrils flare as though he's reading something from the smell of the coin still just lying there in the palm of my hand. "From the bottom of the well. It's an old, old wish. Very potent."

"Wish? You mean like a magic wish?"

He nods.

I hold it out to him again. "So, don't you want it?"

He doesn't speak for a long moment, then finally says, "You've done enough already, helping me out the way you did. Don't you think you earned my help with all the work you did?"

"But it was fun," I say.

And it hadn't felt like work. My chores back home—*they* always felt like work. This had been totally different.

"Which," Hedley says, "is as good an argument as any that you should always try to find employment doing something you enjoy."

"You know what I meant."

"I do. And I repeat, you did enough. If you give me that coin, I'll be so far in your debt that I might never be able to repay you."

I look down at the coin in my hand. If it's worth *that* much, why did Mina just give it to me?

"I don't think it's me so much as Mina you'd owe," I say. "Is that it?"

"It's more that Mina already feels she owes me a great deal—a feeling I don't share, I might add—and this is her way of trying to repay her imagined debt to me."

"This all sounds way too convoluted and complicated," I say.

"I suppose you might see it that way."

"So she was trying to trick you into *really* going into her debt?"

"I don't think so, but that would be the end result."

"I don't get it. I mean, a wish is just a wish, right?"

He shakes his head. "You know the stories, don't you?"

"Sure. You mean like, the guy throws a fish back into the sea, and the fish turns out to be magic and gives him three wishes."

"Exactly. He did the favor first, and the wishes were given to him to repay that favor. But if you take the wish first, then where are you?"

"Um . . . owing a favor?"

He nods.

"And that's bad because?"

"I value my freedom," he says. "I don't want such a debt hanging over my head."

"I get it. And you think Mina would want you to do something you didn't want to do."

"Not necessarily. But you don't know, do you? I'm not one to speak ill of anyone, but the simple truth is you don't want to be indebted to a fairy. We can be . . . devious, with little care for others."

"Mina said she wasn't a fairy."

"She's not. But she's lived as one for long enough that, willy-nilly, tricksiness is in her blood."

"So I should just give this back to her because it'll only work for you, and you don't want it."

He shakes his head again. "No, it will work for anyone."

"But then they'll be indebted to her."

"Now you have it. Until the debt is paid, you will carry its weight. And then, when you *are* called upon to discharge it, the deed you're asked to do might be an even heavier weight to bear. So you see, it's nothing I want to burden myself with. Life is short enough as it is without our making it harder on ourselves with so-called shortcuts like wishes."

"Yeah," I say. "And I wouldn't want that, either."

I stick the coin back in my pocket.

"Thank you," he says. "Are you ready to go?"

He folds his apron and sticks it under the counter. I follow suit and put on my coat. I wrap my leftover pie in its napkin and stick it in my pocket.

"All set."

"We'll go quicker if you ride on my shoulders."

I give him a dubious look.

"I won't drop you—though you'll have to duck your head, from time to time."

So that's how we go, Hedley walking at a good pace with me perched on his shoulders, my bag banging against my side. We wave good-bye to the stragglers still tidying up their stalls, then Hedley opens a door I hadn't noticed before and we go up a flight of stairs—not the ones I took to get here, but just as steep and seemingly endless. On the plus side, all I have to do is clutch the collar of his jacket and peer around, instead of making my own way up. I still can't figure out where the light's coming from, and when I ask Hedley, he says they're fairy lights, as though that explains it all.

I guess it does.

"Littles keep to themselves," Hedley says in a low voice when he finally stops. He stoops to let me down, adding, "But I know there are tribes living in the buildings on either side of us and no underground routes connecting them. The only way to visit from one to the other is by flying, or using this alleyway."

I slide from his shoulders onto the ground and look about. The alley we're in doesn't look a whole lot different from the dozens of others we've already come through on the way here from the Goblin Market, but I figure Hedley knows what he's talking about. At least he has so far.

"So we just wait?" I ask.

He nods. "But quietly," he says, still pitching his voice low.

He sits down on a stack of flattened cardboard boxes that are tied together with twine. I pull my coat a little tighter around my throat—the temperature's dropped again—and lean with my back against the stack, my bag on the ground at my feet. I still have tons of questions, but I just try to follow his lead and stay quiet.

I think of what he said about how Littles keep to themselves. I know it's like that out where I live, but that's only because travelling—even from house to house—is a major undertaking and dangerous, too.

I didn't think it was like that in the city, but while I was in the Goblin Market, I saw any number of small beings—people, fairies, and a lot of who-knows-what-they-ares—but not a single Little. I haven't since Mina brought me into the city in her cat carrier.

And then I do.

I hear the creak of wood squeaking and turn to a low window in the building across from where we're sitting. A Little has pulled aside a bit of window frame to slip outside. Now he pushes it closed behind him with another creak and steps up to the bars that guard the window. They'd keep even a small child from getting in or out, but a Little can just slip between them, easy as pie. I have to smile. One afternoon in Hedley's stall and already I'm thinking in bakery clichés.

"Excuse me," Hedley says in a quiet, polite voice.

The Little freezes, all except for his gaze, which darts across the alley to lock onto the gnome. I'm sure he's about to bolt—just like I knew exactly the moment the cat was going to pounce on me, back in the field yesterday—but then his gaze moves to me, and I see a momentary indecision.

"Hi!" I call out, lifting my hand to wave at him.

"Please don't be alarmed," Hedley adds. "We only wish to ask you for directions."

The Little plays it smart. He doesn't disappear back into the building, but he does stay behind the bars.

He's one of the more human, less birdlike-looking Littles, not exactly handsome, but he's got a rakish air about him. I figure he's in his late teens, and he's wearing clean, what look like machine-made clothes and a pair of sneakers—all taken from some Barbie and Ken doll set, I'm guessing, or something similar. I had a pair of sneakers like he's wearing once, but they wore out. I never did make myself a pair of cargos that look as good as the ones he's got on.

He points to me.

"Come over here," he says.

"Why should I?"

"Because I want to see if you can."

I look at Hedley, but he only shrugs. So I push away from the stack of cardboard and cross the alley. When I get to the window, the Little offers me a hand. I hesitate a moment, then reach up. He lifts me easily, but that's a thing about Littles. We're all stronger than we look, and with our light bird bones, we don't weigh much. Lots of times, Littles can take quite a tumble and be no worse for the wear than a few bruises, maybe a broken arm or leg if we land really wrong. I know—my uncle. But when he fell off the table; he'd had the bad luck to land on his neck and break it. Otherwise, he might have survived.

"You see?" I tell the Little. "No one's forcing me to do anything. Hedley's a friend. He's not going to hurt you or me or anyone else."

"He's a gnome, and gnomes can be dangerous."

"So can Littles," I say.

I reach behind my back as I speak. Before he has time to react, my knife's in my hand and pointing at his belly.

He holds my gaze for a long moment, then shrugs.

"I'm just being careful," he says. "A Little's best defense is not being seen."

"I know, I know. But I'm telling you that Hedley's okay. He's a baker-slash-ratcatcher, except he doesn't kill rats. He just talks to them and convinces them to go somewhere else."

"Handy."

I nod. I put my knife away, pull my pie from my pocket, and unwrap it. I have a bite, then break off a piece and offer it to him.

"This is one of Hedley's pies," I say.

He takes a bite, and I watch the pure joy fill him as he tastes it.

"That," he says, "is unbelievably good."

"I know. And you could get some any weekend at the Goblin Market, where you don't have to worry about being seen because there's a truce there, and let me tell you, six-inch-tall people are the least weird thing you'd find wandering around."

He gives a slow nod. "My name's Jan," he says, holding out a hand.

"I'm Elizabeth. Do you want to come meet Hedley?"

He waits a beat, then smiles. "Sure. Why not?"

We jump down to the ground and walk over to where Hedley's still sitting on the stack of cardboard boxes. When we get near, Hedley offers a finger, and he and Jan shake.

"What kind of directions do you need?" Jan asks.

"We're looking for a Little named Jenky Wood," I say.

"Well, you won't find him here," Jan tells us. "He's gone south. With the winter coming on, all the bird Littles have gone south."

"But . . ."

"Think about it," Jan says. "Why stay here when you have the wings to take you to someplace warmer?"

"Then why haven't you got some wings and gone yourself?" Hedley asks.

He shrugs. "Well, I'm happy being who I am. I don't want to go flying about in the air as a bird. And you know, it's not all you might have heard it to be. There's those that change and can't change back. And then there's been those who change back, but at the wrong time—when they're hundreds of feet in the sky and there's nothing in between them and the ground but car exhaust and air."

I swallow, still hating the picture that puts in my head.

"Hedley mentioned that," I say.

Jan nods and stamps a foot on the ground. "This is where I want to be. Standing on my own two legs."

"So they're all gone," I say.

"That's right. But you don't need one of those bird boys if you're on a pilgrimage to get your own wings. All you have to do is go to the Place of Change, though why you'd want to, I have no idea."

"Place of Change?" I ask.

"It's what the tribes have taken to calling the apartment of the woman who showed Jenky the trick of changing."

"You mean Sheri Piper's home?"

"Someone's been doing her research."

I don't bother explaining how I know.

"Can you take me there?" I ask.

He nods. "I can take you close enough to point out the building, but I won't go in myself."

"Because you're—" I was going to say scared, but I don't want to insult him. "Because you don't want to change yourself?"

And besides, it's not like I've gone all courageous myself. But I can't have come this far and not at least have a look at the place.

"Like I said," Jan tells me, "the change is a bit of a crap-shoot. There's no way to tell how it will work out for you until you actually try it. I don't see it being worth the risk."

"That's okay," I say. "I wouldn't ask you to."

"Do you want me to come with you?" Hedley asks.

I do. But I also want to get word to T.J., and that seems more important. The only danger I'm in here is going to come after I go into Sheri Piper's apartment—*if* I even do.

I explain that to Hedley, and he nods.

"I'll talk to your friend," he says. "The fact that I'm a

gnome won't make her nervous or frightened?"

"Are you kidding? She'll love it."

He offers me his finger to shake then, just like he did with Jan, but I'm feeling sentimental and step closer to give him a hug. He bends down so that his whiskers touch my cheek for a moment, then he straightens up.

"Take care of yourself," he says. "It was nice to meet you, Jan."

He tips a finger against his brow, and then I let Jan lead me off. We walk halfway down the alley to where a narrow old coach lane leads off between the buildings and turn into it.

"He's not like I expected," Jan says.

"What do you mean?"

He shrugs. "I don't know. He was just so polite. I didn't think fairies were like that."

"I didn't even know they existed for real until this morning."

He gives me an odd look. "What street have you been hiding on?"

"I'm from north of the city," I tell him.

"Really? Then you're the first country Little I've heard of to make the pilgrimage."

"That's only because no one told us that the change is real."

"Oh, it's real," he says. "It's just not the smartest—"

"I know, I know. I'm with your program. But I still want to see for myself."

He nods, but I'm not sure he believes me. I'm not sure

I believe myself. I know there's a huge risk. But there's the possibility of so much freedom to be had as well.

"You don't have any more of that pie, do you?" he asks.

I smile and pull what's left of it out of my pocket, break it in two, and hand him half.

It's funny, isn't it, how you can be so at ease, never realizing the way it can all go wrong in the blink of an eye.

Hedley waits until the Littles have rounded the corner and are out of hearing before he turns to the heap of garbage bags piled up against the side of a Dumpster that looms over where he's sitting.

"Well, little man?" he asks the shadows behind the garbage. "Will you help me in this?"

Something stirs in the darkness, then steps out into the dim light of the alley. It's a diminutive man, not much taller than a Little, with small dark eyes widely set in a long narrow face. He's dressed all in gray, and when he stands still against the pavement, he seems to merge with the asphalt, almost disappearing from sight.

"I wish you wouldn't call me that," the small man says.

He has a bristle of stiff hair on his upper lip that stands out like whiskers and moves when he speaks.

Hedley smiles. "I'm not going to start calling you King Rat. You're not *my* sovereign."

"It's only a speaking name."

Hedley has no idea why his companion pretends to a humble stature when his constituency numbers in the hundreds of millions. They are his eyes and ears, a vast array of unloved, unwanted creatures. Rats, pigeons, and flies. Cockroaches, sparrows, and starlings. Squirrels, mice, and other rodents. They aren't necessarily the most handsome or powerful of followers, but it's impossible to deny the sheer weight of their numbers.

Unless you're the odd little man who calls himself King Rat.

"Of course it is," Hedley says. "And Tatiana McGree's only a humble fairy, rather than the queen of all the city's courts."

"Then call me Gogol," the little man says.

Every time they speak, King Rat has a new name to offer up.

"Writing your memoirs, are you?" Hedley asks.

"I believe Gogol was more of a novelist."

Hedley shrugs. "Gogol it is then. For today. Can you help me with this?"

"For the usual fee?"

King Rat has a sweet tooth—especially for Hedley's pies.

"Of course," Hedley says. He gives his companion a considering look. "Now, I'm curious. Naturally, I'm delighted to have your help—so handily at my disposal—but I can't help wondering what it was that brought you to this alley?"

"I heard something about a coin. . . ."

"Ah."

"A wish, I was told."

Hedley nods. "It's only Mina, trying to pay off a debt that doesn't exist—except in her mind."

"But it's a wish."

"It is, indeed. And a potent one, too. Perhaps the Little will give it to you."

King Rat nods. "Perhaps."

"And then you'll be in Mina's debt."

"Maybe, maybe not."

"And maybe you're her sovereign as well, and then that wish would only be a part of her fealty to you."

"Oh, you do have an imagination," King Rat says, then changes the subject. "I heard the Little helped you out today at your stall. What happened to Juyeon?"

"She never came to the market today. Do you know why?"

"I could find out—for the usual fee."

Hedley smiles but shakes his head. "I'm sure you could, but it's not that important."

"Not if you already have a replacement."

"I don't think I do," Hedley says. "Moon knows, Elizabeth has both the temperament and the talent, but she wants to fly."

"Ah. She's one of *those* Littles."

Hedley knows what his companion is thinking. "Those Littles" were either doomed, or they went away, flying high and free in their new winged shapes.

"So why are you helping her?"

"I don't know. I liked her. I liked her innocent humor

and heart. And besides," he added, "I'm curious to meet a human that a Little would trust."

King Rat nods. "There's not many of those, and no wonder, considering."

"We're certainly in agreement with that." Hedley glances down the alley in the direction that the Littles had taken before looking back at his companion. "How long will it take for you to find this human?"

King Rat shrugs. "Not long. She lives north of the city?"

"In the new developments."

"The birds around there have nothing to do but gossip. So we'll start with a Little in the company of a dog and work back from how your Elizabeth and he met. Their meeting won't have gone unnoticed. It's not the sort of thing my people . . ."

He breaks off at Hedley's smile.

"Your people?" Hedley asks.

King Rat frowns, then continues as though he hasn't heard. "Nothing goes unnoticed, and the more unusual, the easier it is to remember. So . . ." He squints one eye as he calculates. "Maybe an hour?"

"I'll wait to hear from you."

"Where will I find you?"

Hedley smiles. "With all those eyes at your command, I wouldn't think you'd need to ask."

King Rat makes a disgusted sound, but he smiles, too.

"One day you'll call me by my name," he says.

And by doing so, name King Rat as his sovereign.

Not likely, Hedley thinks. But instead of bringing that up, he simply says, "And one day you'll admit to its meaning."

"Who knows?" King Rat says. "Anything's possible— or at least, so I've heard."

Then he slips back into the shadows and is gone.

Hedley glances again in the direction that the Littles had taken. He wishes there was something he could have said to convince Elizabeth that it's always better to make do with what you are, rather than try to become something you aren't. But who was he to decide for another?

And what did he know? He'd never really wanted to fly.

Viva Vega

≸≸≸≸≸≸≸

T.J.'S LEGS FELT way too shaky. Her heart pounded in her chest, like it was trying to escape the cage of her ribs. She glanced around the field, trying to keep her gaze on the boy who seemed to have appeared out of nowhere, but also trying to see if there were any more of his gang around.

He seemed to be alone, but that didn't make her feel any less anxious.

"Don't—don't you try anything," she told him.

"You need to chill, *chiquita*. I'm just standing here, okay?"

Oh God, oh God, oh God, T.J. thought. What was she going to do?

"I've got a gun," she told him.

That was stupid, but it was the first thing that came to her mind.

"Yeah, sure you do."

Though her eyes had adjusted to the darkness again, she couldn't really see his face clearly. But she could hear the smile in his voice.

"And I've got a nice new shade of lipstick here in my pocket," he added. "Just take it easy. I'm not here to hurt you."

"Then why are you here?"

She saw him shrug. "It wasn't right what we did this afternoon. I was feeling bad about it, so I thought I'd see if I could collect your stuff and get it back to you."

"Yeah, right."

That got her another shrug. "Think what you want, *chiquita*. I know what's true."

T.J. wished she could actually see his face, though she wasn't sure why that would help. People were really good at lying and not showing it—just look at politicians. But still, while he didn't seem to be a threat, she didn't trust him for a moment.

"Why do you keep calling me that?" she asked.

"Calling you what?"

"*Chiquita.*"

"I don't know your name."

"It's T.J.," she said before she realized that maybe she shouldn't be telling her name to some bully she didn't even know. Didn't even *want* to know.

"I'm Jaime—Jaime Vega."

She almost expected him to put out his hand, but he just stood there, looking at her. Then, when he did finally reach out, he had her cell phone in his hand.

"I got this back from them," he said as she took it. "Your other stuff should be around here somewhere, except for the money that was in your wallet. Ricky kept that."

"Who's Ricky?"

"Ricky Thompson."

The name alone didn't help T.J. place him. But she could tell her brother, and when Derek tracked down this Ricky Thompson, he'd be sorry.

"I tried to stop them," Jaime said.

"I didn't see you doing anything when you were all pushing me around."

He ducked his head. "Yeah, I know. I don't feel good about that. But I meant after—when they were going through your stuff."

"Why do you hang around with people like that if you say you're not like them?"

"Who am I supposed to hang out with?"

"I don't know. I'm new. We just moved here this summer. Before that we lived on a farm outside of Tyson."

"Yeah, well, I'm new, too," he said. "They readjusted the school districts over the summer so that instead of me being able to go back to Redding High with my friends, I'm stuck here in Mawson with all you rich kids. And you know what really sucks? Ours is the only house on my street that's in Mawson's district."

"I'm not rich," T.J. told him.

He shrugged. "You know what I mean. Around here everybody's got an iPod, and most of them seem to have their own cars."

"I don't even have a CD player," T.J. said, "but I can play music on my computer."

"Whatever. That's not the point. The point is I'm shut

off from my old friends, and the only people who give me the time of day are Ricky and his buddies, and even they rag me about my dad being a landscaper instead of the CEO of some big-ass company. But I'm proud of my dad."

T.J. still couldn't see his features, but she could tell by the way that he stood that he was just waiting for her to challenge him, to say there was something wrong about his dad's job.

"I grew up on a farm, remember?" she said. "I don't see anything wrong with landscapers—or even gardeners, for that matter."

"And I suppose you're totally cool with Hispanics."

"Not when they're mean like you."

"I told you, I—"

"Didn't do anything when your friends were bullying me. Right. I remember that. And for your information, I worked side by side with the workers my dad hired at harvest time. Most of them were from Mexico and the Caribbean, and I got along fine with *them*."

"Aw, crap, this is coming out all wrong," he said. "I'm just trying to say I'm sorry."

"You're not really. You're just trying to justify being a bully."

T.J. wasn't sure when it had happened in this conversation, but somehow she'd gone from being scared to just feeling annoyed.

Jaime stood there looking at her, then he ducked his head again.

"Yeah," he said. "I guess you're right. So let me just say I'm sorry and leave it at that."

T.J. nodded. "Okay. I'm still kind of mad at you, but thanks for coming back to tell me that."

"I didn't do such a great job of it."

"And I totally understand what it feels like to be left out," she went on. "My brother Derek makes friends really easy, but I'm not so good at it. Everybody around here seems to be . . . I don't know. Kind of shallow. Like it's all about stuff and who you know."

"Welcome to the real world."

"I guess."

"C'mon," he said. "Let me help you find your backpack."

"That's okay. I already got it this afternoon. I found everything except for my cell."

And a six-inch-tall girl—you didn't happen to see her, did you?

"Then what are you doing here now?"

"I . . ."

T.J. didn't know where to begin.

"I had this teddy bear . . ." she started.

"Yeah, what was up with that? Aren't you a little old to be carrying around a teddy bear?"

"It wasn't like that. It was . . ."

Time for the ferret story again, she realized, but she was sick of that stupid story, and sick of lying to people, and anyway, what did it matter if she talked about Littles? No one was going to believe her, and it wasn't like Elizabeth had stuck around so that she could find her. She was still really worried about Elizabeth, but all this had happened because she'd been going to the bookstore for Elizabeth, to help her solve *her* problems. All T.J. had gotten in return was being swarmed, having her stuff stolen, and then having some old perv trying to drag her off into his car.

"There was somebody inside the teddy bear," she said.

"Some*body*?"

T.J. nodded. "A little girl our age, except she's only around six inches tall."

Why was she telling *him* this? If she was going to tell anyone, it should have been Julie. Or Geoff.

There was a long moment of silence before Jaime said, "What are you smoking, and do you have any more of it?"

"I don't do drugs."

That got her another pause in response.

"Yeah, me neither," Jaime finally said. "But, c'mon. What did you have hidden inside the teddy for true?"

"I just told you."

"Yeah, you did. But let's get real. A tiny girl? You've got to know how that sounds."

"I don't care what you think," T.J. said.

And the odd thing was, she really didn't. At least, not right now. Maybe on Monday morning, when her previous anonymity in the school halls changed to snickers and fingers pointed behind her back—there's the girl who believes in fairies—maybe then it'd be different. But right now it felt liberating.

"And now," she added, "I'm going home because it's too dark to see properly, and I'm never going to find her anyway."

"Okay," he said. "I get it. You're playing with my head because I was such an asshole. But now I really just want to help."

"I'm not making anything up, and I really don't care what you think."

"Yeah, but—"

"I have to go now."

"Then let me walk you home," he said before she could turn away.

T.J. didn't care anymore if he knew where she lived or not, but that didn't mean she was suddenly going to be best friends with him. He was still one of the kids who'd pushed her around and stolen her stuff—even if he had come back to say he was sorry.

"I've got my bike," she said.

"So you can walk your bike. I'd feel better seeing you home. You never know who you might run into at this time of night."

"I think the only thing out here I have to be worried about is you."

"I won't say you're not cute, but I'd never try anything unless you wanted me to. If it makes you feel better, you can keep your bike between us and ram me with it if you think I'm going to try something."

What kind of something? T.J. wondered. Maybe a kiss

like Geoff hadn't? Because just as had happened with Geoff, she could tell that Jaime was interested in her, even with her crazy story about Elizabeth.

What was it with today? She'd had no friends, period, since moving here, and now suddenly she had *two* boys making nice to her?

And why was he still acting all helpful? Didn't he think she was a complete mental case? Or maybe he did, and he was just humoring her.

It was all too complicated, so she just shrugged.

"Whatever," she told him.

And this time she did turn around and start back to where she'd left her bike. He fell in beside her.

"You're limping," he said after a few moments.

"Yeah, that's what happens when people push you around and you fall down."

"Aw, man. Those guys are such jerks. *I'm* such a jerk."

"You are."

There was nothing he could say to that.

She kept expecting him to go away, but he stayed with her as she collected her bike, walked through the bookstore parking lot, and came to Crestview Driveway. There was no traffic now—just some taillights going off into the distance, into the city.

They crossed over and started up Rosemary Lane.

"I'm going to tell my brother about you guys," T.J. said.

"Is he a tough guy?"

"He's tough enough. And he's got friends."

"Good. A brother should stand up for his sister."

T.J. glanced at him. "Aren't you going to ask me not to tell him about you?"

"Why should I? I was there. I was part of it. The difference between me and the other guys is, I'm not going to put up a fight. I deserve to get my ass kicked."

T.J. really didn't get why he would hang around with this Ricky Thompson and his friends. Jaime seemed like a good guy. He had a bit of a chip on his shoulder, but she supposed that would happen if you were treated badly for long enough.

"Was it really so bad for you coming to Mawson High?" she asked.

"End-of-the-world bad."

She nodded. She understood that. It was exactly the way she'd felt, losing Red, leaving the farm, having to go to this new school with everybody already knowing everybody else, all the cliques formed and their ranks closed to newcomers unless they had some particularly special level of coolness to offer.

"At least you can still go back to your real home," she said.

"I guess. But they treat me differently in the neighborhood. Now the other guys all act like I'm one of you—I mean, one of them. The rich kids."

"They don't sound like they were very good friends."

He shrugged. "That's just how it goes. They all hang around together at school. By the time I make the hike back from Mawson with my sisters, they're already off, doing their own thing. I don't blame them. I just don't seem to fit anymore."

"Except with Ricky and his crowd."

That got her another shrug. "I don't really fit with them, either."

No kidding, T.J. thought. The longer she spent in his company, the more she liked him. And the less it made sense that he'd be with those bullies.

"But they were someone to hang with at school," he went on. "And I guess it just grew into after school, too. But it's not a great place for me to be. Most of the time, I feel like I'm a pet."

That woke a guilty twinge in T.J. She remembered Elizabeth being so adamant about not wanting to be anybody's pet. She supposed you didn't have to be as small as a Little to have that feeling.

"Well," she said, "you could always have lunch with me."

"Right. After your brother's kicked my ass."

"This is my street," she said.

They turned off Rosemary and started up the incline.

"Maybe I won't tell him about you," she added.

"Why not?"

"I think you feel bad enough already."

"I don't need—"

"Anybody's pity," she said before he could finish. "Yeah, I figured that much. You're a tough guy. But maybe I'm not doing it just for you. Maybe I'd like some company, too."

When he didn't say anything, she turned to look at him. She suddenly felt awkward, and that she'd gone too far. She didn't know what had come over her. She was too shy at school to make friends, and she'd never been particularly outspoken at home. But here she was, practically propositioning some guy that she hardly knew anything about except that, first impressions to the contrary, he seemed decent. His good looks—now that she could see his features more clearly under the streetlights—didn't hurt, either.

He was going to think she was such a loser.

But if he did think that, he was hiding it behind a smile.

"How old are you?" he asked.

"Fifteen. Well, almost fifteen."

He nodded. "I'm sixteen. I guess it's true what they say about girls maturing quicker than guys."

"What do you mean?"

"I don't know. It's just . . . I like the way you talk and think. It's not all giddy and goofy like my sisters. Don't get me wrong—I love my sisters. But they can drive me crazy sometimes. You're just . . . I don't know. You're cool."

She *was*?

T.J. had to duck her head to hide a blush, but then they entered the short stretch of darkness between streetlights, and he couldn't see.

"So tell me," Jaime asked, "why were you carrying around a toy-sized girl in your backpack?"

T.J. shot him a look. "Are you making fun of me now?"

"No, I'm just curious."

"But you don't even believe me."

He shrugged. "But let's say you did have a toy-sized girl. What were you doing with her?"

"We were going to the bookstore to meet this writer named Sheri Piper. She writes about Littles—that's what Elizabeth's people call themselves."

"Original."

T.J. smiled. "And they call us Bigs."

"Which would make sense, considering. So why did you want to meet this writer?"

"She's written books about Littles—storybooks—but we thought maybe she might know more, like where we could find other Littles."

"Because . . . ?"

So then T.J. explained how running away hadn't worked for Elizabeth, but that her family had left and they were trying to find them, or some other Littles.

Jaime nodded when she was done. "You've worked it all out."

"Worked all what out?"

"This story of yours."

"I *knew* you didn't believe me."

"Would you believe a story like that from someone you'd only just met?"

"I'd . . . I'd . . ." But T.J. had to shake her head. "No, it sounds crazy."

"I don't know about crazy—or at least not lock-her-up-in-a-straitjacket crazy—but you have to reach pretty far to try to make any sense out of it."

"I guess. But just because you haven't experienced something, that doesn't mean it's not real."

"That's true." He smiled. "So for now I'm going to keep an open mind."

"Really?"

"Sure. I can't see any reason for you to make up something like that."

T.J. stopped rolling her bike.

"This is where I live," she said.

Jaime looked at the house. "It looks nice."

"I guess. I preferred our farmhouse back home. But who knows? Maybe one day we'll move back to the country. We're only renting this from a woman where my mom works—she got transferred to California for a couple of years."

Jaime nodded. "You don't have to make excuses. I know how the world works. Some people have stuff, other people don't. It's no big deal."

T.J. wanted to say that she hadn't been makeing excuses, except she supposed that's exactly what she'd been doing.

"Maybe I'll see you in school on Monday," he said.

"Sure."

"It was nice talking to you."

He lifted a hand in a casual wave, then turned around and started walking back down the street. T.J. wanted to call after him but stopped herself. She had nothing to say.

The only reason she didn't want him to go was because she'd been enjoying their conversation, too.

She watched his figure recede, stepping in and out of the pools of light cast by the streetlights. She wondered why she'd told him about Elizabeth when she hadn't told Geoff. Maybe it was because it had been dark and so late at night and it felt like they were sharing secrets. Though mostly, she supposed, it was because she was sick of lying.

She stayed on the street until she couldn't see him anymore, then wheeled her bike back across the lawn to the back door of the garage, worried that every little noise would make her parents appear, demanding to know what she was doing out at this time of night.

But when she'd made it safely back to her bed, the alarm clock set to go off in just a few hours, her thoughts turned to neither Jaime nor Geoff. Instead, she stared at the ceiling and worried about Elizabeth.

"Oh, I don't know," T.J.'s mother said the next morning when T.J. asked her parents if she could go to the Sheri Piper signing with Geoff. "After what happened yesterday . . ."

"*Mom!*"

"We don't know this boy at all and—you said he was, what? Eighteen?"

"Seventeen."

"That still seems a little old for you," her father said.

"I already told Mom," T.J. said. "We're not dating. God. He's just giving me a lift to the signing."

"But still . . ."

"Then can you or Dad drive me into the city?"

Mom sighed. "T.J., you know we're going over to the Rouds' today. We've had it planned for a week."

"Maybe Derek can take you," her father said.

Derek shook his head. "I have band practice."

"It's just to a bookstore," T.J. said. "In the middle of the day."

Her parents exchanged glances.

"Well, maybe if we can meet him first," her father said.

T.J. smiled. "I know you're going to like him."

The signing at the downtown Barnes & Noble wasn't exactly in the middle of the day—more like the late afternoon—but Geoff hadn't minded coming over before her parents had to leave for the Rouds' house. He arrived early so that they could assure themselves that he was just a nice guy who worked in a bookstore, not some psycho-killer-rapist lusting after their precious teenage daughter.

Dad quizzed him on his plans after graduation, which T.J. knew was to point out how at the end of this school year Geoff would be going away to university while she was still sitting in a classroom in Mawson High. Mom, thankfully, kept her lioness claws sheathed. She acted interested and polite, though she did study him intensely whenever he wasn't looking, as though memorizing his features for some future police artist's sketch. Derek left just as Geoff was arriving and offered up only a simple hello and a look of sympathy.

And, happily, Geoff didn't bring up her "pet ferret."

When they were finally alone, T.J. and Geoff remained at the kitchen table, where they talked about books and movies until it was time for them to leave themselves.

"I don't think your parents liked me much," Geoff said as they pulled out of the driveway.

It was the first comment he'd made about them. When T.J. had apologized for their intense scrutiny earlier, he'd simply shrugged it off.

"They liked you fine," she assured him.

"Then how come your mother kept giving me those hard stares?"

"Don't worry about it. She'd do that even if you were the Prince of Wherever and had a thousand references. And don't forget—they *did* actually leave us alone in the house."

"I suppose." He glanced at her before returning his gaze to the road. "So how are you holding up? After yesterday, I mean."

"I don't know. I guess what gets to me is the randomness of it all. There was no reason for those boys to attack me, or for that man to grab me. It just happened."

"Wrong place, wrong time."

T.J. nodded. "But at the same time it doesn't *feel* that simple."

"What does it feel like?" Geoff asked when she fell silent.

"It's stupid."

"Try me anyway."

T.J. sighed. "Okay. I know it's not true—honestly, I do—but it feels like it was still my fault, somehow. How dumb is that?"

"Not very. You're just trying to make sense of it, but because there *was* no sense to it, that seems to be the only thing that does make sense."

"What are you planning to major in—psych?"

He shook his head. "No, I just read a lot."

They fell silent for a while, Geoff concentrating on his driving, T.J. staring aimlessly out the window.

Where are you, Elizabeth? she wondered. Did we just drive right by the place where you're hiding? Did you see me in a car with a boy, like I'm going out on a date, and figure I've just given up looking for you?

"It's funny," Geoff said after a few moments of silence. "One of the hardest things to get our head around is that we just don't meet very many real villains in our everyday life. In books and movies, we know who the good guys and the bad guys are, but it's not so easy to tell when we close the book, or step out of the theater."

He glanced at her and she nodded to show she was listening.

"It seems to me," he went on, "that when we have trouble with people, it's not because they're evil, but because they're mean-spirited, or spiteful, or just stupid. I'm not saying it's necessarily any less dangerous than coming face-to-face with a storybook villain. It's just that their motivation is . . . I don't know. Kind of base."

"So I guess your major's actually going to be philosophy," she said.

Geoff smiled. "I guess none of that's particularly comforting, is it?"

"No, I think I know what you mean. It's all really shades of gray."

"That's exactly what I meant."

T.J. looked out the window for a long moment.

"I met one of those guys last night," she said finally. "One of the gang that swarmed me."

"You *what?*"

"But the thing is, he seemed nice. He was really apologetic. Apparently, he was going back to the field to collect my stuff to bring it back to me."

"What were *you* doing there? Oh, right. Your ferret. What was her name again?"

"Elizabeth."

Now was the moment she could admit she'd been lying and tell him the truth. It hadn't gone so badly with Jaime.

"Except she's not really a ferret," T.J. said.

"Oh?"

He looked over at T.J., eyebrows raised.

"I just said that," she went on, "because I didn't think you'd believe me if I told you what she really was."

Oh, boy. This was a lot harder in the middle of the day, riding in a car as they drove along industrial parks and strip malls, heading into the city. It had been so much easier in the dark. And maybe not just because of the dark. Last night she'd also been ticked off with Jaime and hadn't really cared what he thought.

"So, what is she really?" Geoff asked.

"A girl. A little teenage girl around six inches tall."

Geoff smiled. "Yeah, right."

"No, really."

He glanced at her, then cursed as a car cut them off. He tapped the brakes, concentrating on his driving for a moment, before he looked at her again.

"I get it," he said. "We're going to see Sheri Piper, so you're pretending you lost a Little yesterday."

"I *did* lose a Little."

He shook his head. "Come on, T.J. You're in high school now."

"What's that supposed to mean?"

"That you should act your age and not make up crap like this. Maybe it's cute back in the sticks where you came from, but it doesn't cut it here."

This was exactly how she'd expected it to go when she'd told Jaime last night.

"Jaime believed me," she said.

"Who's Jaime?"

"The guy I met last night when I went back to look for her."

"He told you that?" Geoff asked. "He actually said he believed you?"

No, T.J. thought. But at least he'd said he'd keep an open mind about it.

But she just said, "Yes. He did."

Geoff shook his head. "He just wants to get into your pants."

"No, he's just more understanding than you obviously are."

"Oh, for God's sake. And I suppose you were going to tell Piper this, too?"

"We were going to see her because Elizabeth's on her own, and we thought maybe she could tell us where we could find other Littles."

"Buy her books. That's the only place you'll find them."

"Why are you being so mean?"

"Why are you being so stupid?"

"I . . ." T.J. felt a burning behind her eyes, but she refused to cry. "I'm *not* being stupid," she said. "You just have a closed mind."

Geoff suddenly turned the car into the parking lot of a strip mall. He stopped it, parking diagonally across a couple of empty spaces, and put it in neutral before he turned to look at her.

"I'm going to save you a lot of embarrassment," he said, "and just take you right back home again. Sheri Piper probably has little kids coming up to her all the time who think that her stories are real, but you're fifteen. You're supposed to be a little more mature than that by now."

"But—"

"Honestly, what do you think she's going to say? 'Oh, yes, it's all real. It's such a relief to finally meet someone else who's seen them?' It's not going to happen. She'll be polite, I'm sure, but she's not going to tell you anything that you don't already know yourself: Littles and fairies and ghosts and monsters aren't real. And anyone who thinks differently is only lying to themselves."

"Screw you," T.J. told him.

She opened the door on her side and started to get out.

"Hey, wait a minute," he said.

He grabbed her arm, but she pulled free and stepped onto the pavement.

"You're not my babysitter," she told him.

"Yeah, but maybe you need one. I'm responsible for you. What are your parents going to say?"

"Why do you care?"

"Will you just look around yourself?" he said. "This is not an area where you should be on your own."

It wasn't. It was the middle of nowhere, where Highway 14 had become Williamson Street, which would eventually take you all the way into downtown and finally, to the lake. But here it was all strip malls and car shops, liquor stores and pawnshops. It was still north of the urban blight called the Tombs—block upon block of abandoned tenements, factories, and office buildings—but it wasn't a great neighborhood.

"I'm still going to the signing," she told him.

"I can't leave you here."

"I don't care what you do."

He frowned, then gave a reluctant nod. "Okay. I'll take you to the bookstore."

"I'm not getting back in that car with you," she said. "You're just going to turn around and take us back to the 'burbs."

"I promise I—"

But she slammed the door and started for the nearest bus stop. She could see it on the next block, in front of a liquor store. There was an old pickup truck parked in its lot, along with a very cool chopper—all chrome and shining steel, with extended handlebars. T.J. wasn't particularly enamored with the lifestyle most people associated with this kind of motorcycle, but she loved the look of the machines themselves.

She turned around when she heard Geoff get out of the car and start to follow her.

"Stay away from me," she told him.

"Or what?"

"Or . . ." She reached into her pocket and took out her cell phone. "Or I'll call the police and tell them that you're harassing me, and they'll lock you up."

She hadn't figured out yet how to tell her parents that she'd gotten her phone back last night, so it was still deactivated. But he didn't know that.

"I'll tell them you believe in fairies," he said. "You're the one they'll lock up."

"I'll tell them I don't."

"Oh, for God's sake, T.J. Will you just get back into the car?"

He started toward her, stopping when she held up the cell.

"I've got 911 on a speed dial," she said. "All I have to do is push one button."

She turned away again and continued to the bus stop. Checking over her shoulder as she went, she saw Geoff trailing along behind her.

"C'mon, T.J.," he said as she neared the liquor store.

She held up the cell again and pointed it at him when she stopped under the sign for the bus stop. Jaime's friends had stolen her money yesterday, but her father had given her twenty-five dollars this morning so that she'd have some money for her trip downtown. She just hoped that bus drivers made change, because she wasn't about to go into the liquor store to ask them. She probably wouldn't even be let inside the door.

Geoff had stopped again as well. He stood a dozen or so feet away from her now. His frustration was plain, but he was trying to hide it with a smile that never reached his eyes.

"We don't need to do this," he said. "Just come back to the car, and I'll drive you to the bookstore."

She shook her head. "I don't trust you anymore."

"Goddamn it!" he shouted. "Would you quit screwing around?"

At that same moment, the door to the liquor store opened and the owner of the motorcycle stepped out with a six-pack dangling from one hand. At least T.J. assumed the motorcycle was his. He was tall and broad-shouldered, with slicked-back dark red hair, dressed in faded jeans and a black leather jacket, the sleeves pushed up, showing tattoos on either forearm.

He looked from T.J. to Geoff.

"This guy giving you a hard time, miss?" he asked.

T.J. didn't know what to say. He looked so tough. If she said yes, was she just putting herself into an even more dangerous situation?

"Look, we're fine," Geoff said.

The biker gave him a hard look.

"Did it look like I was talking to you?" he asked.

"No, it's just—Jesus, T.J. . . ." Geoff turned an unhappy face to her. "Can't we just go?"

"Miss?" the biker asked her.

Okay. He looked really tough. And the knuckles of the hand that was holding the six-pack were scabbed and red, like he'd been hitting a brick wall. But he seemed very polite.

"I'm just trying to get to a book signing downtown," she said, "and he's gone all weird on me."

The biker nodded and turned his attention back to Geoff. "Take a hike, pal."

"But . . ."

"Don't make me come over there and explain why throwing your weight around your girlfriend is *such* a bad idea."

"She's not my—"

"Don't care. I just want to see you walking away."

Geoff gave her one last pleading look, but T.J. had made her decision now. When she shook her head, Geoff turned away and started back to his car.

"Do you have money for the bus?" the biker asked.

She nodded. "Um, do you know if bus drivers make change?"

He smiled. "I couldn't tell you the last time I took a bus, sorry."

Over his shoulder she could see Geoff getting into his car. He started it, but he didn't pull back out onto the street. The biker glanced back.

"You want me to stick around until the bus shows up?" he asked.

"I don't want to impose. . . ."

God, he was being really nice. It just showed you that you really shouldn't judge people by appearances. Of course, that didn't mean he couldn't turn all weird the way Geoff had. She certainly hadn't expected it from Geoff.

"Or I could give you a lift," the biker went on. "You can wear my helmet, though it might be a little big on you."

"I . . ."

God, her parents would kill her if they found out, and they would find out because Geoff would tell them. Geoff would spin the whole story so that it looked like she'd gone crazy, which, talking about Elizabeth and Littles the way she had, it would seem she was.

"It's cool," he said. "We can just wait for the bus."

T.J. nodded. There was something familiar about him, but she couldn't figure out what.

"How'd you hurt your hand?" she found herself asking.

He lifted his hand to show his knuckles. "This?" He smiled. "It's not like you might think. I've got a garage a couple of blocks over, and I was just working on a car when the wrench slipped. Bashed my knuckles against the manifold."

"Did it hurt?"

"Like a son of a—" He broke off. "Yeah. It did."

"My name's T.J."

He nodded. "I caught that. I'm Red."

As soon as he said his name, T.J. remembered where she

knew him from. There was this ad for Red's Autoworks that ran all the time on local TV. It started with a guy—Red, here—riding a horse across a big field, but then it changed into him riding a motorcycle and pulling up in front of his garage. He'd take off his helmet and there'd be a close-up with him saying, "Service you can trust," before the camera would pan back to show the garage again, and you'd hear a horse whinnying just before the fadeout. She loved the ad.

"I've seen your commercial," she said. "I really like it."

He smiled. "Yeah, I like it too. And business has picked up."

"Is that your horse in the ad?"

"Nope. But it's my bike. The horse belongs to some friends of mine who live out on the Rez."

"I used to have a horse called Red," she said. "Back when we lived on the farm." Then she realized how that might sound. "I mean, I really liked him." Okay, that sounded worse and kind of flirty, and he had to be, what? At least thirty years old. "I mean . . ."

"It's okay," he said, smiling. "I get what you mean. So, what happened to your Red?"

"I had to give him up when we moved to the city."

His gaze went to his motorcycle, and he shook his head. "Losing your ride—that's harsh. I don't know that I could deal with it."

"It's been hard," she said.

And then the tears she'd held back when Geoff made

her feel bad earlier came pushing at the backs of her eyes again. One slipped out and trickled down her cheek.

"I . . . I'm sorry," she said, wiping it off with a sleeve. "Sometimes it just hurts all over again."

Red gave her arm an awkward pat. "It's okay to cry. Shows you're real."

"I guess. . . ."

She looked past his shoulder again to see Geoff still sitting in his car, watching them.

"Maybe . . . maybe I will take that ride," she said.

Red turned to give the car a look as well, then he led the way to his bike. He stowed the six-pack in one of its saddlebags and handed her his helmet.

"I've got a smaller one at the shop if you want to make a stop on the way," he said.

She nodded. "You shouldn't be riding without one."

"I'll give you an amen to that."

It wasn't the law here, but that didn't mean it was smart to ride without a helmet.

"You ever ride on a bike?" he added.

"No."

"Well, there's nothing to it. Just hang on and take your cues from me on which way to lean into the corners."

"Okay."

He cocked his head, a smile in his eyes. "We can still just wait for the bus."

"No, this is good. I really appreciate it. You've been so nice."

He gave Geoff another look, then shrugged.

"I don't like bullies," he said.

Then he started up the bike, and they were off.

Geoff banged his fist against the dashboard. This was unbelievable. First that crazy story of hers, and now this. And no matter what T.J. thought, he *was* responsible for her. If anything happened to her, he was the one her parents were going to blame. What the hell was she thinking, riding off with some greasy biker?

He didn't know why he'd ever offered to drive her downtown in the first place.

No, that wasn't true. She was cute, and he'd felt bad for her after what had happened to her yesterday. But he should have known better because she was so damned young. Who knew she actually believed in fairies and crap like that? He could just imagine Sheri Piper's face when T.J. started talking about them to her.

Geoff put his arms on the steering wheel and laid his head against them.

What was he supposed to do now? Follow them? That biker would notice and probably come back and beat the crap out of him. But if anything happened to her, he was going to be the last person to have seen her safe. *He* was the one who'd let her ride off.

Maybe *he* should call the police, except what would he say? Neither T.J. nor the biker had actually broken any law. He couldn't call her parents, either. No, that wasn't true. He could, but they weren't home. He wasn't about to leave a message on their answering machine about how their daughter had taken off to go joyriding.

He was still trying to decide what to do when the motorcycle showed up again, coming back up the street that it had turned down earlier. This time they were both wearing helmets.

Geoff sighed with relief. Okay, maybe this wasn't so bad. They looked his way, then the biker gunned his machine and they headed off down Williamson Street. If they stayed on it, the street would take them right downtown to the bookstore.

While they were still in sight, he pulled out onto Williamson himself, heading in the opposite direction. He was sure that the biker would note that in his rearview mirror. Except he wasn't going home. Instead, he drove a few blocks over to Flood Street and took it downtown. Since it was a less-used thoroughfare—especially on a Sunday—he'd probably get to the bookstore before them.

Maybe he'd be able to get T.J. alone and talk some sense into her before she made a complete fool of herself.

Maybe not.

But he knew this much for certain: one way or another, he was taking her back to her parents' house.

"Think your friend'll show up here?" Red asked as he pulled his motorcycle up to the curb near the entrance to the Williamson Street Mall.

T.J. got off the bike and shook her head.

The bookstore where Sheri Piper was doing her signing

was inside the multistoried building that rose up at the end of Williamson Street, overlooking the lake behind it. Thirty years ago, it had been the first big and modern mall in the city—*the* place to shop. But with the exodus to the 'burbs in the last couple of decades, most people started going to the sprawl of big-box stores and suburban malls. It was only in the past few years that the Williamson Street Mall had begun regaining some of its former cachet.

"I don't think so," she said. "But even if he does, there's lots of people here, and I can't imagine he'd start anything."

She'd enjoyed riding on the back of Red's motorcycle more than she thought she would. The feeling of that powerful machine under her reminded her of riding on the tractor back home—but the speed was more like riding her own Red. She wondered if her parents would let her get a motorcycle when she was old enough to get a license. Right. As if.

"That was *so* cool," she said.

"Yeah, nothing beats a bike. You should try it out in the country where you can really open it up."

"You sound like the way I used to feel riding my horse," she said. "Like you're free."

Red nodded. "That's the word. Freedom."

T.J. looked at Red's motorcycle, admiring the shine of the chrome, the sleek lines.

"Someday I'm going to get one," she said.

"A bike?"

T.J. nodded, and happily he didn't treat her like some dumb kid.

"Look me up when you're ready," he said. "I'll make sure you get a good machine for your money."

"Maybe I will."

"And you'll be okay getting home after?" Red asked.

She nodded. "My folks'll be home soon. I can call them to pick me up."

"Okay. But take this anyway, in case you need a ride or anything."

He gave her a business card that said "Red's Autowork" and his name, William Ford. Under the text was a drawing of a motorcycle just like his, with the garage's address, phone number, and e-mail underneath it. Red had added another phone number in ballpoint.

"That's my cell number," Red said. "Try it first because I'm not going back to the shop today."

"Thanks. I don't think I'll have to, but if I need to, I will."

"Okay. Take care, T.J."

"You, too, Red," she said.

She smiled. It was so weird calling a *person* that.

She watched him drive away before she turned to the mall entrance. She'd been here before with her parents and knew that the bookstore was up on the second floor. The second and third floors, actually, since it had two levels.

She hesitated before going in. She was remembering the fight she'd had with Geoff and couldn't shake an uneasy feeling.

Yes, she had all these memories of a tiny six-inch-tall teenage girl, but what if she really *had* imagined everything to do with Elizabeth? Didn't that make much more sense than the idea that Littles could be real? People got messed up—you heard about it all the time. They heard voices, or saw things. And they never knew they weren't real.

So what if Geoff was right?

What if she needed help, but it was help with being crazy, not help from the author of a bunch of kids' books who might not even listen to her anyway?

If someone was to ask her for concrete proof, she had absolutely nothing to offer. All she had were her memories, and if they were wrong . . .

She couldn't go there.

She'd never questioned her memory before, and she couldn't start now, because that *was* acting crazy. She knew what she knew, and anyone who didn't believe her . . . that was their problem. She decided she disliked Geoff even more than she had earlier in the car for making her question herself like this.

Squaring her shoulders, she started toward the mall entrance.

There was a sign just inside the door advertising the signing, with a picture of Sheri Piper and her latest book. T.J. studied the picture. Piper looked so young in this photo, but T.J. knew that looks could be deceiving. Lots of times they used old publicity pictures with the author looking ten years younger, if not more. But Piper had a nice face. Her eyes seemed kind, with just a hint of mischief.

Feeling a bit more confident, T.J. took the escalator up to the second floor, then walked to the front of the mall to the entrance of the bookstore. A clerk gave her directions to the children's-book section, where the signing would take place. It was up on the third floor, but this time she took the stairs instead of using the store's own escalator.

It was a good thing she did, because as soon as she stepped around an aisle and was about to cross over to the children's section, she saw Geoff standing at the top of the escalator. Worse, he had a mall security guard standing beside him. She ducked back into the aisle.

Oh, God, now what? She couldn't believe he was here. And *what* had he told the security guard?

"So who are you hiding from?" a voice asked from behind her.

She turned so fast she almost fell into the bookshelf beside her, and might well have, if Jaime hadn't put out a hand to steady her.

"Gee, thanks a lot," she told him. "Now I know what it feels like to almost jump out of my skin."

Jaime smiled. "You're welcome."

"It wasn't meant as a compliment. What are you doing here? Have you been following me?"

"I didn't have to. You told me you were coming here today."

"But why are *you* here?"

"Maybe I couldn't wait until Monday to see you again."

"Oh, right."

"Why's that so hard to believe?" he asked.

"I don't know. It's not, I guess. I just . . ."

She shook her head, then turned to peek around the

corner of the bookshelf again. Geoff and the security guard were still standing at the top of the escalator—just far enough back so that they wouldn't be noticed until you were already committed to riding up.

"I didn't think you had it in you," Jaime said when he had a look himself.

"What's that supposed to mean?"

He shrugged. "I don't know what you did, but you're obviously hiding from that rent-a-cop."

"I didn't do anything," T.J. told him. "It's that stupid Geoff standing beside him."

She ducked out of sight again and sat on the floor, back against the bookshelf. Jaime followed suit, and she gave him an abbreviated version of the afternoon's events.

"I didn't say I believed you, either," Jaime said when she was done.

"No, but you did say you'd keep an open mind. And you didn't make fun of me and treat me like some immature little kid."

He gave her another shrug.

"Well, it meant something to me," she said.

"I didn't mean it like that. It's just . . . what am I supposed to say? People don't talk about that kind of thing unless it's true, or they're crazy, and you don't look crazy to me, so I'm keeping that open-mind thing going."

"See, Geoff was totally *not* like that."

"So, what are you going to do?" Jaime asked.

"I don't know. I didn't come all this way to not see Sheri Piper."

He nodded. "Yeah, I want to check her out, too."

"I didn't know you were into books."

"Hey, I can read."

"I'm sorry, it's just . . ."

"'S cool. Like I said. I wanted to see you again before Monday. But I also want to see what's up with these Littles."

"Except as soon as I step out there," T.J. said, "that security guard is going to bundle me off somewhere and hold me until my parents can get here."

"Not if you play the stalker card."

"What do you mean?"

Jaime nodded with his head. "This Geoff guy. Just go out there and freak out all over the place that he's always following you and hitting on you and why can't he get a life instead of being some pathetic loser."

"I couldn't do that."

"Sure, you could. You just take how angry he made you, and put it on this made-up thing instead of on what really happened. It's not like he cut you any slack."

"I don't know. The security guard's never going to believe me."

"C'mon, it's two of us against one of Geoff. And if the rent-a-cop still wants to get all stupid, refuse to go anywhere until they bring the store manager."

"But—"

"Don't forget: *you* haven't done anything wrong. You're just here to see this lady writer."

Jaime stood and pulled T.J. to her feet.

"I'll be right beside you," he said.

"You really think I can do it?"

He smiled. "T.J., you can do anything you put your mind to. That's what my dad always says to me."

"Your dad calls you 'T.J.'?"

Jaime gave her a soft punch on the shoulder. "Yeah, and he tries to get me to wear dresses, too."

Picturing Jaime in a dress was just silly enough to make T.J. laugh, and laughing made a lot of her nervous energy drain away. Jaime took that moment to put his arm around her shoulder and steer her out from behind the book-shelves.

"And the dresses he pulls out," Jaime went on. "They're all frilly and lacy. Not even my sisters would wear them."

T.J. giggled.

And then suddenly the security guard and Geoff were in front of them. T.J. stepped out from under Jaime's arm and let her gaze go to Geoff. It wasn't hard to feel angry. She was still furious with him for the way he'd treated her.

You just take how angry he made you, and put it on this made-up thing instead of on what really happened.

"Excuse me, miss," the security guard said. "But I'm going to have to ask you to—"

"God, you are so pathetic," T.J. told Geoff. "Do you have to follow me everywhere? I am so going to get my dad to have a restraining order put on you."

The security guard frowned. "Miss . . . ?"

"And who are you?" she asked him. "The stalker's apprentice?"

"Um, miss? If you'd just come with us . . ."

T.J. glared at the security guard. "I am not going *any-where* with you and that creep." She looked around, raising her voice. "Where's the store manager?"

"This young man works for the store," the security guard said.

T.J. turned back to him. "No, he doesn't. He works in the store on Crestview Driveway, which is why I can't go into that store, because whenever I do, he's all over me."

"That is such a lie," Geoff said.

T.J. ignored him. "Where's that store manager?" she asked the guard. "I'm here for an author's reading, and I don't want to miss the beginning."

The security guard looked from T.J. to Geoff, obviously feeling very uncomfortable.

"T.J.'s father is a lawyer," Jaime told the guard. "He specializes in libel cases."

"He . . ." The security guard had to clear his throat. "He said you were acting crazy and that your parents had put you in his care."

"Acting crazy?" T.J. repeated. "You mean, like, following him around wherever he goes, or parking outside of his house all night? I wonder where he'd get ideas like that."

The security guard nodded. "I'm sorry to have troubled you, miss."

"Wait," Geoff said. "You can't believe this—"

"I'm sorry," the guard told him, "but I'm going to have to escort you out of the mall."

"But—"

"I don't care what you told me," the guard said, "but she's right. The only person with a crazy story here today is you."

"Look, I never stalked—"

"I don't know if you did or didn't. But you're the one causing a problem here today, not her. So I need you to leave. Now, are you going to come quietly, or do I have to call for backup?"

Geoff turned to T.J. "Look, I'm sorry, but—"

"You should be."

"The things you were saying . . ."

T.J. shook her head. "I don't know what you're talking about." She turned to the security guard. "Can we go to that reading now?"

"Of course. I'm sorry to have troubled you."

She and Jaime watched as the guard walked Geoff to the down escalator. It wasn't until they were on it and going down that she realized how much her legs were shaking. She had to hold on to the balustrade.

"That was amazing," Jaime told her. "Have you ever thought of becoming an actress?"

T.J. shook her head.

"Well, maybe you should."

"Yeah," T.J. said. "It's just great finding out how good a liar I am."

"You weren't lying. Well, you were, but it was for a good cause, and he started it. This was payback, T.J., plain and simple."

"It still doesn't feel very good."

"That's because you're a good person—not a liar like Geoff."

"But he doesn't think he was lying. He thinks I'm crazy." She gave Jaime a pained look. "And what if I am?"

Jaime blinked in surprise. "What?"

"Well, doesn't talking about little miniature people qualify as being crazy?"

"Where's this coming from?" Jaime asked.

"I don't know. Everything's kind of weird and awful right now."

"Do you want to skip the reading?"

"I . . ."

She was about to say, "Yes. I think I do." But then she saw a small blonde woman riding the escalator up to them. It was Sheri Piper, and she looked *just* like her photo, right down to the kind eyes.

She stepped out of Piper's way, then turned to watch her walk over to where the store had set out a bunch of folding chairs, about half of which were occupied. Walking beside Piper was a tall, dark-haired woman in a smart suit, but Piper herself was dressed casually, the way you'd expect an artist to be dressed. Cowboy boots, a knee-length skirt, a casual shirt, a leather jacket folded over her arm. In her free hand she carried an artist's portfolio.

"Is that her?" Jaime asked.

T.J. nodded.

"Why didn't you say anything to her?"

T.J. shrugged. "I guess I want to see what she has to say first."

"Well, let's grab a seat," Jaime said.

He took her hand and gave her a little tug to where the chairs were set up.

T.J. was so absorbed in Sheri Piper's presentation that she didn't even think to have a look around to see if Geoff might have come back, or if the security guard was checking them out. She was barely aware of Jaime sitting so close beside her, his chair right up against hers.

Piper showed paintings from her earlier books, and then some sketches for the new book she was working on, which was about a mouse named Henry. She read from the book that she was promoting today—a story about fairies living in an alleyway who were losing their homes as their neighborhood got gentrified. And then she answered questions from the audience members, most of whom seemed to be nine or ten.

T.J. didn't ask any questions herself. She thought a lot of them were silly, little-kid questions—like what were Piper's favorite colors? or where did she get her ideas?—except T.J. discovered she was just as interested in the answers as anyone else, so maybe they weren't so silly after all.

Then it was time to line up to get books signed.

T.J. didn't have a book herself and didn't want to use the money her dad had given her in case she needed it to get home. But she and Jaime lined up all the same. When it was finally her turn to stand in front of Piper, T.J.'s mouth suddenly felt too dry and her legs had gotten shaky again.

"No book?" Piper asked her.

"I . . ."

"That's okay. I'm just happy you came out to see me. Would you like a bookmark?"

She had a stack of them on the desk, an image taken from the current book, T.J. realized.

"No," T.J. finally managed. "I mean, yes, thank you. But I was just, um, wondering if after you've, you know, you've finished signing and everything, if I could, um, just talk to you for a moment. Sort of privately—if that would be okay, Ms. Piper."

Piper smiled. "Please, call me Sheri. What did you want to talk about?"

"Um . . ."

T.J. shot a glance at the kids still in line behind her.

"If it's about reading a manuscript," Sheri began, "I'm sorry, but I don't really do critiques."

"No, no. It's just . . ."

This was so much harder than T.J. had expected it to be—especially standing here in a line with the kids behind getting impatient because she was taking up so much of Sheri's time.

Sheri smiled again and took pity on her.

"Just wait until the line's gone," she said, "and we can take a moment."

"Oh, thank you."

She moved away from the table and sat down at the end of the front row of chairs. Jaime took a couple of bookmarks before he followed and sat down beside her. She stared at the floor, not wanting Jaime to see how embarrassed she was feeling, but looked up when he gave her arm an awkward pat.

"Can you believe how dorky I sounded?" she said.

"Hey, you did fine," he told her. "It's a tough deal to try and lay it all out in just a couple of minutes."

"I know—but, God. I was so tongue-tied."

"She seems nice," he said. "And it'll be better when you don't have a whole gang of kids waiting for you to finish."

T.J. nodded. "She *is* nice," she agreed.

She tried not to watch to see when Sheri would be finished with her readers. But finally the last little boy turned from the table, his signed book held against his chest as his father led him away. A store clerk came up to the table with a stack of books from a nearby display, but Sheri stood up.

"I'll sign those in a moment," she said.

And then she was walking over to where T.J. and Jaime sat. Jaime got up to offer her his seat, but Sheri got a chair out of the row and pulled it around so that she could sit facing them.

T.J. took a deep breath. Okay. It was now or never.

She'd been rehearsing how she'd begin ever since she'd left the signing table, trying out all sorts of different ways to ease into what she needed to say. But now that the moment was here, all her planning went right out of her mind.

"I've seen a Little," she found herself saying. "No, that's not quite right. For the past few weeks, I've had a Little for a roommate."

Oh, God, was that the stupidest thing to say, or what?

But Sheri only gave her a long considering look, before she asked in a mild voice, "What was his name?"

T.J. blinked. That was the last thing she'd expected Sheri to say. No, that wasn't true. The whole reason she'd made the effort to see the writer was because she hoped that Sheri knew they were real as well. But T.J. had never actually believed that would be the case.

"He's actually a she," T.J. said. "Her name's Elizabeth— or at least that's what she calls herself. Her real name, so far as I can tell, is Tetty Wood."

"Like in my book," Sheri said.

T.J. gave her a blank look until she remembered that the Little in Sheri's first book had been named Jenky Wood.

"I don't think they're related, though who knows? She has a brother named Tad, but I don't know her parents' names. They all moved away when Elizabeth ran away from home and we met."

"Maybe you should start at the beginning," Sheri said.

So T.J. did.

Sheri didn't say anything when T.J. was done. The silence only lasted for a few moments, but it felt like forever and T.J. couldn't stand it.

"You do believe me, don't you?" she asked.

"I don't quite know what to say," Sheri replied.

"C'mon, Ms. Piper," Jaime put in. "Just look at her. Is that the face of a liar? I don't think so."

"It's just Sheri," the author said absently. Then she gave

Jaime a thoughtful look. "Have you met Elizabeth as well?" she asked.

He shook his head. "I'm the designated open mind."

She smiled. "It's funny the things we get into when we like someone, isn't it?"

Jaime ducked his head, but not before T.J. realized he was blushing.

Sheri looked back at T.J. and said, "I don't know that I can really help you just now. The Littles have mostly gone south for the winter."

"They migrate?" T.J. asked.

"They do now—since they got their wings back."

Jaime looked from one to the other. "So everything in these books of yours is really true?"

She smiled. "So far as I know it is."

"But Elizabeth and her family can't turn into birds," T.J. said. "She thought it was just a story."

"Well, the funny thing is, they have to make a pilgrimage to my apartment, because that's the only place the transformation magic seems to work." Before T.J. could say anything else, she added, "But that's not the real question now, is it? You need to find Elizabeth."

T.J. gave a glum nod. "I'm so worried about her. But I guess there's nothing we can do except hope she's going to be okay."

"We could go back to the field in the daytime," Jaime said.

"I guess." T.J. looked at Sheri. "I was just so hoping that you'd be able to help."

"Maybe I can. Not all the Littles have gone south. Only the ones that can change into birds. We might be able to contact one of the ones that stayed behind." Sheri looked at her watch. "I need to sign some stock and then I have an interview, but if you could meet me at my place in an hour or so, we can see if we can find someone."

In an hour, T.J. thought. It was already almost six. That meant they couldn't even start to deal with her problem until seven or later. She'd have to call her parents to tell them she was going to be late, and how was she supposed to explain what would be keeping her? But she didn't see that she had a choice. If there was any chance that they could find Elizabeth . . .

"Here," Sheri said, offering T.J. a card. "That's got my address on it. It's only a subway stop away. There's a coffee shop just down the street from the station where you can wait if you get there before me. I'll look in to see if you're there before I go home."

"I really appreciate this," T.J. said.

Sheri nodded. "I know what it's like getting caught up in the lives of Littles. How could I not help you?"

"I'm just glad you believed me."

"After a while in this business," Sheri said, "you develop a pretty good B.S. detector. Now I have to sign those books." She stood up. "I'll see you in an hour or so."

T.J. and Jaime both stood up as well.

"I guess I need to find a phone to call my parents," T.J. said as they watched Sheri return to the signing table, "though God knows what I'm going to tell them. Can I borrow yours?"

"I don't have one," Jaime said, "but I saw a bank of them downstairs when I was coming in."

T.J. couldn't remember the last time she'd used a pay phone. She glanced at Jaime, realizing he'd been right last night. Maybe her family wasn't in the same financial stratosphere as so many of her classmates, but they lived well. Her cell phone might not be working at the moment, but at least she had one.

They walked over to the escalator, but before they could start down, T.J. saw a familiar figure getting on the up escalator on the other side of the store.

"Oh my God," she said. "It's my dad!"

She quickly stepped back. Accompanying her dad she'd seen Geoff and the security guard who'd stopped them earlier.

"That little weasel," Jaime muttered.

He grabbed T.J.'s arm and steered her toward the stairs.

"Go," he told her. "I'll head them off."

"But—"

"Just do it. I'll meet you at the coffee shop after I get away from them."

T.J. knew there was no time to argue. She had to go now, or her father would see her. If she wasn't in sight when he got to the top of the escalator, then there was no one to say that she had or hadn't seen him. But if he spotted her and called to her, there would be absolutely no excuse not to face the music. Then she wouldn't be able to meet with Sheri. Then she couldn't help Elizabeth.

There was no question what she had to do.

"Thanks," she told Jaime.

She bolted for the stairs. Since she didn't hear her name being called, she assumed she hadn't been seen. She took the stairs two at a time, arriving breathlessly at the bottom, but she didn't wait to catch her breath. Instead of making straight for the store exit, she wove her way along the side of the store, through the art and travel and biography sections, until she could slip out the front door. She paused there for a moment to look back, then hurried for the escalator that would take her down to the street-level stores.

Here goes nothing, Jaime thought as he sauntered to the top of the up escalator.

He was pretending to be browsing through the stacks of remaindered books on a nearby table when he heard Geoff's voice.

"That's him! That's the guy that was with her!"

A moment later he was confronted by the three of them: T.J.'s father, Geoff the Weasel, and the security guard, who had the decency to look uncomfortable about it all. Geoff grabbed his arm.

"Where is she?" he demanded.

Jaime looked down at where Geoff held him.

"You want to lose that hand?" he asked.

He kept his voice pleasant, but he supposed there was something in his eyes, because Geoff quickly let go and stepped back.

"Please, son," T.J.'s father said. "Where's my daughter?"

"You mean T.J.?"

When her father nodded, Jaime shook his head.

"I don't know," he said. "On her way home, I suppose. We went to the signing, then after it was over, she said good-bye and left. I'm surprised you didn't see her on your way in."

"She went home?" the father said.

"I guess. Where else would she go?"

The father looked at Geoff. "But he said . . ."

"*Oye,*" Jaime broke in. "I don't know what's going on here, but I do know that this guy's not exactly the kind of person I'd be letting my daughter go out with."

"We're not going out," Geoff said.

"What do you mean?" the father asked.

Jaime shrugged. "He didn't tell you how he dumped her in Upper Foxville so she had to make her way down here on her own? I don't know about you, but *I* wouldn't want to be wandering around that part of town without a couple of buddies, and I can take care of myself. But to just leave a fifteen-year-old girl there to fend for herself?" He shook his head. "Man, that's low."

Both the father and the guard turned to look at Geoff.

"You did *what?*" the father demanded.

"I didn't dump her. She got out of the car and wouldn't get back in. And then she took off with some biker. She went crazy."

"She didn't go crazy," Jaime said. "She was just mad at you for tearing a strip off her. And I'll bet you didn't tell Mr. Moore *why.*"

"Look," Geoff said, turning to the father. "She was

saying that fairies and little people were real. I didn't want her to embarrass herself telling Ms. Piper that."

"Aw, c'mon," Jamie said. "So what? She's fifteen. My little sisters think that unicorns and the tooth fairy are real, but I don't go all postal on them."

"That's not what—"

"Why don't you just admit that you treated her like crap and she wouldn't take it?"

"Is this true?" the father said.

Jaime was pleased to see the protective anger growing in his eyes.

"No," Geoff said. "Well, sort of, but it's not like you think."

"And what do I think?"

Geoff looked away and couldn't face him.

"And you," the father said to Jaime. "Why didn't you stop her from leaving by herself?"

"Why would I? She's just taking the subway home."

"You could have gone with her—made sure she was all right."

"C'mon," Jaime said. "We don't exactly live in the same zip code, do we? And anyway, I'm heading over to my cousin's place and that's way over by the Projects."

"So what were you doing here with her?" the father asked.

Jaime shook his head. "I wasn't with her. We go to the same school. We ran into each other and decided to check out the reading together. She went home when it was done. End of story." He made a point of looking at his watch.

"And speaking of heading out, it's time I was gone."

"But . . ."

"*Oye*," Jaime said. "So far as I know, there's no law against hanging with someone you meet at the mall."

He looked to the guard for confirmation.

"You told me Mr. Moore was a lawyer," he said.

"I was yanking your chain. It's not like you were being all that nice to us." Jaime looked back at the father. "I'm out of here," he said. "If I were you, I'd just head on home and wait for her. Nothing's going to happen to her—unless she happens to run into this weasel again."

He jerked his head in Geoff's direction, then headed off for the down escalator. The weight of their combined gazes lay heavy on his back, but no one tried to stop him. He checked his watch again. There was still time to hook up with T.J. before Sheri Piper was supposed to meet them.

T.J. got turned around once she reached the ground floor of the mall. She was in such a hurry to escape her father that she exited through a different door from the one she meant to take. It was dark outside, and she was so focused on putting some distance between herself and the mall that she was almost three blocks away before she realized the mistake she'd made.

Or at least she thought she'd made a mistake—easy enough to do, considering how she hardly ever came downtown and had never been here by herself.

She stopped at the next intersection and looked around. Here it was, Sunday evening, and it was still so busy. It seemed as though most of the stores were still open and the streets were filled with buses and cabs and other vehicles. Sidewalk vendors still had their tables and blankets out, laden with watches and jewelry, CDs and DVDs, scarves and purses. Most of the food carts were gone, but there were still people selling espressos and lattes and chai tea.

It was never like this back home on a Sunday night. But then it was never like this back home, period.

She tried to figure out where she was. The street names were no help because, beyond Williamson, she was unfamiliar with most of them.

She looked left, then right, and that was when she knew she'd taken the wrong exit from the mall. The lake was on her right, when it should have been on her left. She looked back the way she'd come. Retracing her steps would mean she'd have to risk being spotted by Dad or Geoff.

Geoff.

She couldn't *believe* he'd actually called her parents. But now wasn't the time to be worrying about that. She had to get to the other side of the mall without being seen, and quickly enough so that she wouldn't miss meeting up with Sheri.

Going back through the mall was out. Making a detour wasn't the best of ideas, either, since the blocks were long in this part of the city and there was also the chance that her dad might be looking for her.

That left the boardwalk along the lakeshore. It was perfectly safe in the day time, but now that it was dark, T.J.

was a little less sure of how safe it would be. A lot of kids hung out along the boardwalk at night—"the wrong kinds of kids," as Mom would say. The kind who smoked dope and tagged buildings with graffiti.

Probably, nobody would bother her. She'd be just another kid. Except Elizabeth was right. She *did* look like a Goody Two-shoes. The kind of kid that bullies were automatically mean to.

She wished Jaime was with her, instead of back at the mall. She was pretty sure nobody would bother her if he was here. But if she was on her own?

Yesterday was still very fresh in her mind.

She hated this feeling. She'd never been scared back home. Sure, there were tough kids and fights at her old school, but it wasn't the same. And out of school, nobody'd ever tried to bully her or Julie.

She looked back one more time down the street she'd just come, then set off down the block toward the boardwalk, trying to slow the quickening of her pulse. There were people who could sense fear in the way animals did. She'd just have to look brave, though how she was supposed to do that, she had no idea. But then one of the vendors caught her attention.

She was wearing a close-fitting woolen cap with ear flaps, but that wasn't the fun part. The top of the cap had a spiky swath of wool standing straight up from it like a punky Mohawk. The one the girl was wearing was in Rasta colors—orange, yellow, and green—but there were all sorts of different ones on her table, ranging from a plain black to neon pinks and greens.

"Great, aren't they?" the girl said. "They're thirty bucks each, but I could let you have one for twenty-five."

T.J. sighed. That was all the money that her dad had given her, and she needed to keep some for bus fare home. But it was too bad. In the dark along the boardwalk, the cap would make her look like *she* had a Mohawk. The evening was cool enough that it wouldn't be too hot, and it would make her look tougher than she was—or felt.

"I can't afford one," she said.

The girl looked left and right, then leaned over her table.

"It's the end of the day," she told T.J., "and the less I have to carry home, the easier it'll be on me. So tell me, what can you afford?"

"Twenty dollars?" T.J. tried.

"Sold. Which one do you like?"

T.J. dug in her pocket for her money and studied the caps, finally choosing one that was mostly black but had red highlights in the Mohawk. She tried it on, checking her reflection in a store window. It made her smile. In the daytime, she'd probably look ridiculous, but in this light, it looked like she'd been transformed into some punky girl.

"Good choice," the vendor said. "It looks cool."

"Thanks."

Walking away from the girl's table, T.J. felt more confident. She liked the weight of the cap, the look it gave her that she saw reflected in the passing store windows. She could do this. She could walk along the boardwalk with her cap on and a swagger.

She supposed she might never have noticed the pigeon if it hadn't taken flight—its sudden movement in the corner of her eye catching her attention. That was odd, she thought as she watched it flit from one lamppost to another. Didn't birds sleep at night? She smiled. Not in the city, apparently.

She glanced over at it again as she came abreast of where it had landed and was struck by the odd feeling that it was watching her. Not anyone else on the sidewalk, not the traffic on the street. Just her.

Which was stupid, but she couldn't shake the feeling.

What was that dumb movie Derek had made her sit through one night? *The Birds*. Alfred Hitchcock. And it had scared her like nothing she'd seen before or since. It was the horror of something she loved turned ugly and dangerous, which she supposed was why the director had chosen birds. And why all those movies about demonic kids had been so popular for a while. She'd *never* been able to watch them, though Derek and his buddies loved them. They loved any kind of horror movie, the gorier the better.

When T.J. got halfway between the lamppost the pigeon was sitting on and the next one down the street, the bird flew on ahead of her. Its gaze tracked her movement, its head turning to keep her in sight.

Okay, that was just weird.

T.J.

She turned at the sound of her name, but there was no

one behind her. Then, just as she realized that she'd *felt* her name being spoken rather than heard it, she saw the rat sitting on a windowsill, its dark gaze fixed on her.

She shrieked and would have backed right into the traffic on the street, except she banged into a lamppost. A couple of teenage boys walking by laughed but thankfully didn't do more than that. She felt a hot flush of embarrassment. What was she thinking? She'd seen rats before, back on the farm. When the boys had gone by, she looked back at the windowsill. The rat was gone. Of course. It had been more scared than she was.

She turned, her gaze going to the lamppost now. The pigeon was still there, still watching her.

She couldn't help it. The stupid bird just creeped her out. Oh why, oh why did Dad have to show up when he did? If he hadn't, she'd be on the other side of the mall right now with Jaime, the two of them on their way to Sheri's apartment.

She gave the bird a last nervous look, then hurried on down the street. The light was with her and she crossed over, then walked down the steps to the boardwalk that ran along the lake's shoreline. When she looked back a last time, the pigeon was finally gone.

She checked the air and perches nearby—another lamppost, the side of some little building by the water, the tall sign by the railing at the edge of the boardwalk that pointed right to the mall and left to a marina. No bird.

A guy she hadn't noticed rose from a bench. He was skinny, his dark hair a mess, and walked with a slouch.

When he approached her, her pulse quickened.

"Weed?" he asked. "Uppers? What do you want?"

She shook her head because she didn't trust her voice. He just shrugged and slouched his way back to the bench.

Get a grip, she told herself. Just because of what had happened in front of the bookstore yesterday, it didn't mean that the whole world was out to get her.

The hairs prickled at the nape of her neck as she walked by the guy on the bench, but he was staring off into nothing and paid no attention to her.

See? Everything was going to be fine.

She checked the air one last time for the pigeon, then set off at a brisk walk down the boardwalk, heading for the mall. She could see a cluster of kids ahead of her, and her shoulders tensed as she drew abreast of them, but they only looked at her as she was going by.

One of them nodded and said, "Cool hat."

"Thanks."

She started to regain some of her confidence as she left them behind. Ahead of her, she could see the side of the mall that fronted the lake. The huge glass windows loomed over the boardwalk, spilling a bright light that made it feel darker where she was walking. The spookiest thing was how there were these long sections between the lighted lampposts because every second or third one wasn't working. People down here wanted their privacy, she supposed, so they'd broken the lights. It made sense. She'd heard there was a lot of drug dealing—and hadn't that been the first thing she was asked as she stepped onto the boardwalk? There was prostitution, too, if the newspapers were to be believed, but she hadn't seen any indication of it yet.

She kept to a brisk pace so that it looked like she knew where she was going, instead of that she was scared. More than once she caught the sweet scent of marijuana wafting over from the clusters of kids gathered around the benches she passed. She didn't look at them, keeping her gaze straight ahead and ignoring whatever people were doing in the shadows.

That was why she never saw Ricky Thompson until he stepped right into the path in front of her.

"Well, look who's here," he said. "Kind of far from home, aren't you?"

T.J. glanced quickly to either side of him. On the left there was only the railing with a drop into the lake below it. On the right was a bench under a burned-out lamppost. Some kids were gathered around it, but they were already coming out of the deeper shadows to join Ricky.

"Are you looking for your teddy bear?" one of them asked.

"Got any more money?"

They backed her up against the railing, all grins and laughter.

It was too late to run. Too late to do anything except take the beating she knew was going to come. She saw it in Ricky's eyes—that mean look that you'd see in a dog's eyes when it had been raised with beatings instead of affection.

Her throat was thick with fear, and tears pushed at

her eyes. Her knees went weak. She wanted to collapse on the ground. She wanted to beg them not to hurt her, even though she knew that begging would only make it worse, would make them enjoy it that much more. And then she remembered the way Elizabeth would talk to her, telling her to stand up for herself.

And she realized she could. She was mad enough to follow Elizabeth's example. It wouldn't stop them from hurting her, but she wasn't going to just be a victim. The first one that started toward her was going to get a kick, right in the balls. She hoped it would be Ricky. She'd like to hurt him just once before they beat her up.

"I . . . I'm not scared of you," T.J. lied.

It was then that she realized that there were other boys coming up behind Ricky's gang, coming up behind them and approaching from either side. A dozen, maybe more— it was hard to tell in the poor light—had drifted over from where they'd been lounging nearby, slouched on benches, sitting up on the railing that overlooked the lake.

Ricky grinned at the little crowd that was gathering and preened for them.

"Yeah?" he told T.J. "Not even a little bit?"

She shook her head.

"Well, you should be."

If I Had Wings . . .

IT'S BEEN THE better part of an hour since we left Hedley behind in the alley and headed off on our own. During that time we've been sneaking down other alley-ways and creeping through little hidden passages under the streets, not to mention following shortcuts that take us into and out of the cellars of buildings. We seem to stay off the radar when it comes to Bigs—I guess they just don't pay attention to the world around them like a Little has to—but twice we've had to avoid alley cats. They aren't as big as the one that stalked me in the field yesterday. These are raggedy, skinny things with mean eyes. City strays, but completely feral.

But they aren't the worst.

That would be the goblins.

We're walking along an alley, after just exiting yet another building by squeezing through the narrow breach between the window jamb and its protective metal screen-ing. Suddenly, Jan gives me a push back toward the screen.

"Wh—?"

He puts his head close to mine.

"Don't say a word," he whispers in my ear. "Just get back inside."

I hear the faint jingling of small bells as we squeeze back behind the screen. There's some smelly old rag lying there that we stepped over earlier. This time, Jan picks it up and throws it over us. I start to protest, but he hisses in my ear.

"*Whisht.* Not a *word* or we're both dead."

So I crouch down beside him with that horrible cloth on top of us. I shift a little until I can peek through a gap. There's nothing in the alley, but the bells are jingling louder.

"Goblins," Jan whispers. "Coming back from a successful hunt."

"How can you tell?"

"The victory bells. Now, *whisht.*"

I don't want to *whisht.* I want to know more about goblins and victory bells and what kinds of victories goblins celebrate. But I shut up. I figure Jan knows more about the dangers of the city than I do, considering he's lived here his whole life and I'm barely through my first day. And then the goblins come into view, and I'm so glad we're hiding under this smelly rag and keeping still.

They're about twice Hedley's size, which still makes them small by Big standards, but they're as fierce and raggedy looking as those alley cats we hid from earlier. They have blue paint, or blue tattoos, on their brows and cheeks, with long stringy hair and wide faces that seem almost like funhouse mirror reflections. The bells are attached to cloth strips wound around their ankles, and a strong musky odor wafts over from where they're passing by.

The first two are carrying short spears. They're followed by another six carrying a pole from which hangs a dead dog. Bringing up the rear are three more, one with a spear, the other two with short bows and quivers of arrows banging on their backs as they walk.

I don't realize I'm holding my breath until they're finally gone and the jingle of their bells is fading in the distance. Jan sweeps the rag off of us and stands, brushing at his clothes. There's nothing on him, nor on me, but the smell of the rag lingers. Or maybe it's that combined with the stink of the goblins.

"That was just gross," I say, "and I don't even like dogs. Well, except for Rosie, but she's barely big enough to be considered a real dog."

Jan lifts his brows in an unspoken question.

"This feral I know has her as a companion," I explain.

"I didn't know there still were ferals."

I smile. "That's right—I forgot. They call themselves rangers now."

He nods. "We should keep going."

I look down the alley in the direction that the goblins took. It's the same direction we're going.

"Is it . . . will it be safe?" I ask.

"As safe as the city ever is."

So we continue down the alley, then duck into one more of these secret passages that Jan knows. I figure the city must be riddled with them, and I wonder how Jan remembers them all. Then we're outside again, emerging into yet another dark lane between tall brick buildings. At the far end, streetlights create a welcoming glow that we're not going to enjoy because that's not a Little's life, is it? A Little's life is hiding and creeping about and generally doing her best not to be noticed.

Did I mention that I get cranky when I get tired?

I decide to rest for a moment and sit down on a scrunched-up soda can.

"Is it much farther?" I ask.

Jan smiles at me. But he can, can't he? He hasn't had the day I've had.

"Anything worth having is worth the wait," he says.

"I never said I was going to *do* the bird thing. I just want to check it out, that's all."

"You aren't leaning toward it, even a little?" he asks.

"Well, sure. Until I found out how wrong it can go, I was all, where do I sign up?"

"And now you're not."

I shrug. "Now I don't know. I mean, it's tempting." I look at him. "Haven't you ever dreamt you had wings? That you could fly?"

"Sure," Jan says. "But if I was going to have one wish come true, I'd rather be a Big."

"A Big?"

He waves a hand. "Look at this world around us. All the cool things belong to them. The clothes. The music. *Everything.*"

I so can't believe what I'm hearing.

"I know exactly what you mean," I tell him.

"I want to be a musician," Jan says, "but where would I get a real instrument my size? And who'd listen to me? I want to record music and be played on the radio. I want to play concerts."

"I know a guy in a band," I tell him. "Well, I know him, but he doesn't know me. He's the brother of my friend T.J. She's a Big."

He doesn't seem any more surprised than Hedley was, but I suppose city Littles have seen it all.

"What would you play, if you could have an instrument?" I ask.

"I've got a guitar I put together myself," he says. "The body's made from a metal pillbox and it has wires for strings. But it doesn't sound right. I want to plug in. I want to be *loud.*"

I smile. "You sound like me, complaining about having to make my own clothes instead of just being able to walk into some cool store and buy them."

He just looks at me and I realize all he sees is this ratty old coat that Bakro gave me. So I open the coat and show off my T-shirt. It's a little grungy right now, but still pretty cool.

"You sewed that?" he asks.

I nod. "It's all hand-stitched."

"What do you use for the design?"

"Magic Markers that the Bigs leave lying around. But only the waterproof ones—I've learned that from experience."

"It's cool," he says.

He looks away for a moment. I don't know where he goes, but I think it's somewhere in his head.

"See," he adds when he turns back to me, "that's another reason being a Big would be so much better."

I just look at him.

"I don't want to be a parasite all my life," he explains.

That I totally get. It was what made me feel so good this afternoon. I'd been actually earning my own way instead of scavenging and stealing.

"I look at my dad," Jan says, "and I don't know how he can have done this for . . . it must be forty years now. I go crazy when I look ahead and see that same life waiting for me."

"I guess being a Big would be something like flying," I say, "because you'd be able to rise above the scrounging life of a Little. You'd be free to do, to *be* anything you wanted."

"It would be better than that. A bird still has to scrabble for a living. It still has to look over its shoulder every moment to be safe." He shakes his head. "Man, I'd give anything to have been born a Big."

I put my hand in my pocket and feel the coin that Mina gave me. A wish, Hedley called it. Mina'd told me to give it to him, but he didn't want it. I don't want it, either—not after what he told me about the weight of debt you'd bring upon yourself by using it. But if you wanted something as badly as Jan wanted to be a Big, maybe you'd be willing to pay the debt, even if you didn't know what was going to be asked of you. Given the way fairy tales go, it could be any-thing, up to and including your firstborn kid. But maybe Jan wouldn't care.

I'd give anything, he'd just said.

So I almost tell him about the wish, but then I think about how it always goes in the stories. You think you're asking for one thing, but you wind up with something else that makes whatever crap you were trying to escape seem like heaven in comparison. And that's not even counting the debt to Mina he'd incur.

I remember what Hedley said: *Life is short enough as it is without our making it harder on ourselves with so-called shortcuts like wishes.*

So all I say is, "Yeah, being a Big would be pretty cool, all right."

Jan stands and offers me a hand up.

"It's not far now," he says. "Just one more block."

This close and I'm reluctant to go any farther. It all seems so pointless. To be a Little or a bird—as Jan pointed out, it doesn't make much difference. You're still trapped in the life of a scrounger. I knew just what he meant about looking ahead and seeing the years of my life unwinding as a Little. It was why I left home. It was why I'd come to the city.

But I'd already seen that I lacked the essential bravery to make a change. Why would standing in front of the Place of Change be any different?

Besides which, I was pretty sure I don't even *want* to

be a bird anymore. Not if it means the change could be permanent. Or worse, give out on you while you're way up there in the air.

But I let him pull me to my feet. We go the rest of the way down the alley, which takes us out onto a narrow street with cars parked at the curb along either side. The brick houses come almost right to the sidewalk—only their stoops and the little stairwells going to basements separate them from the pavement.

"It's over there," Jan says, pointing. "Across the street."

The brown brick buildings all look the same to me.

"How close can we get before we're . . . you know, affected by the change?"

"You have to go right inside," he says.

"I wonder why it works like that."

He shrugs. "Who knows?"

We wait until a car goes by and check for pedestrians before we cross the sidewalk and jump down from the curb to the surface of the street. Then we follow the curb down the street, the parked cars looming over us, until finally Jan leads me under one of them so that we can cross the street. We peek out from where we're standing beside the front wheel of the car.

"It's clear on my side," I say.

When he doesn't answer, I turn to see him standing with his head cocked, listening. I wonder, what . . . ? Then my pulse quickens, because now I think I can hear the bells, too. Goblins.

Except it's not bells, I realize as I look past him, down

the street. It's the squeaky wheels of a shopping cart that's being pushed by a woman in a dirty pink housecoat with curlers in her hair. I think she's fat until I realize that she's wearing many layers of clothes. Her cart is full of loose pop cans, and plastic bags that are stretched out to their limit, but I've no idea what's in them.

"That's Pop Can Sally," Jan says. "You see her all over the place, collecting her cans."

"I guess Bigs can be scavengers, too," I say.

He nods. "We have to be careful she doesn't see us."

I'm surprised. Bigs rarely look up or down, missing out on whole worlds of activity that are going on around them.

Jan turns and catches the look on my face.

"She'll be looking for us," he says. "See?"

And I do. She doesn't look under every car, but she looks under enough of them to make me nervous. Worse, she has a long stick that she whacks around between the wheels. If she was to do it under our car, we'd both be knocked off our feet and probably killed.

"How does she know about us?" I ask.

I'm trying to be cool about it, the way Jan is.

"She doesn't," he says. "At least not about Littles in particular. She's looking for space monkeys."

"What?"

He smiles, but without much humor. "I think bogles or sprites played a trick on her once because now she thinks that little monkeys from Mars are out to get her. She's always poking around, looking for them, trying to prove that she's not crazy—or at least, not crazy about *that*. The trouble is, the places she looks are where a Little might hide."

"What should we do?"

"Hope she doesn't look under this car. But if she does . . ." He points up into the chassis of the car we're under. "Can you grab that?" he asks.

I don't know what it is. Some cable that's hanging down from the engine. But I nod, because I'm pretty sure I can reach it.

"We'll get greasy," he says, "but she won't be able to reach us up there. Just pray the car doesn't have an alarm, or we'll be deaf for hours."

Pop Can Sally's only two cars away now. I can hear her muttering to herself, but I can't quite make out the words. I don't want to scramble to safety.

"So, what are we waiting for?" I say.

"I'd rather not get all dirty unless I have to."

I can hear the rattle of her stick on the pavement, one car away.

"Not me," I tell Jan. "I think I'd just as soon be greasy and safe."

I jump up, catch hold of the cable, and pull myself off the ground. The *squeak-squeak* of the shopping cart's wheels approach our car.

"Come on!" I cry.

Jan jumps for the cable just as the stick appears under the car. I grab for his arms to help him up, but the sweep of the stick catches his legs and knocks him down. Before he can recover, the stick returns. I hear bones cracking and then he's being slammed against one of the rear tires.

"What's that, what's that?" Pop Can Sally says.

She peers under the car, but I guess she doesn't see Jan's limp body where it lies in the shadow of the tire.

"I know you're somewhere, little monkey man," the crazy woman says. "Don't think I won't find you."

Then she's moving on to the next car. The wheels of her cart go *squeak-squeak* as she moves on. The stick starts to rattle on the pavement one car down. But then that car's alarm goes off, a klaxon *whoop-whoop-whoop* that makes my ears hurt. But all I can do is clutch the cable and stare at Jan's broken body where it lies.

I hear Pop Can Sally's cart go squeaking rapidly down the street, back the way she came.

"Monsters, monsters!" she's screaming in time to the car alarm.

I drop from the cable and run over to Jan.

Somewhere a door opens, and I hear a male voice cursing. But the car alarm dies. Then the door slams shut again and I'm kneeling there beside Jan in the silence.

I don't know what to do.

I stroke his brow and repeat his name, over and over, like it will bring him back. Like it will make him whole again.

I feel him shudder, and his eyelids flutter open.

"I . . . I can't feel . . . my legs. . . ."

Blood trickles from the corner of his mouth.

All I seem able to say is, "Oh God, oh God."

His gaze finds mine, his eyes swimming with pain.

"Guess . . . guess I . . . screwed up. . . ."

"You can't die," I tell him. "You can't. Tell me what to do."

Then it comes to me.

"The Place of Change," I say. "If I bring you there, it can help you, right? It can change you."

"In . . . into a . . . broken . . . bird. . . ."

"We don't know that. Maybe it'll make you whole again."

"Don't . . . want . . . to be . . . a . . . stupid bird. . . ."

He coughs, and a bit of blood sprays onto his chin and chest.

Then my panic narrows to the reminder of what I have in my pocket. Mina's coin. The wish. If I use it, I might just make things worse. If I use it, I'll be indebted to her—and God knows what that will mean.

But if I don't, Jan will die.

I remember what Bakro told me about freeing Rosie.

I did what anyone would do—what anyone should do when they come upon injustice.

I know I can't let him die—not when I have the means to save him in my pocket. It doesn't matter what it costs me.

I take out the coin and hold it tightly in my hand.

How does a wishing coin work?

At a well, you toss it in and make your wish. But there's no well here. There's just me and a dying Little, hiding under a parked car.

So I guess I have to improvise.

I form the wish carefully in my head. Then I take the coin, and I throw it toward the curb.

It clinks against the curb, falls back to the street, and just lies there. Nothing happens.

Crap, crap, crap. That wasn't it.

I start to get up to fetch it again, but then the coin begins to glow.

Bright, bright, brighter still.

Things That Explode
in the Night

WITH HER BACK against the railing, T.J. was all too
aware of the lake behind her, the cold water lapping against
the jagged rocks under the boardwalk. There was no escape
that way—and if she was lucky, Ricky wouldn't simply toss
her over the railing for a laugh. There was no escape to her
left or right either, as kids continued to come drifting over
to check out the situation. And then there was Ricky and
his gang of losers, right in front of her.

"And what's with the gay hat?" Ricky asked. "Is that
supposed to make you look cool or something?"

"Why don't you just leave me alone?"

Ricky shrugged. "Because it's more fun not to. And let's
face it. You're the kind of little girl who's just crying out to
be—"

A large black teenager suddenly stepped out from the
crowd to stand in between them, and Ricky broke off. The
newcomer had a beanie pulled down over his dreadlocks,
but for all the chill in the air, he wore only a T-shirt and

a pair of baggy jeans, slung low on his hips. His bare arms were muscular and covered with tattoos.

"Hey, bro," Ricky said. "You don't need to—"

The newcomer held a finger up in front of Ricky's face.

"First off," he said, "I'm not your brother, and if I was, I really think I'd have to shoot myself."

"Look—"

"And secondly, we have a good thing going here. The cops let us hang out, smoke a little weed in the evening, it's all good. Nobody bothers us if we don't bother anybody. You get where I'm going with this?"

"Not really. I—"

"You're making waves, asshole. Pushing around some kid like you're the King of Shit Hill, but all you really are is just one more turd. You think if you hurt her, it's not going to come back on all of us here?"

"Hey, I was just—"

"So what I need you to do is take your skinny white ass back to the 'burbs and not come back here again, because we don't need you, and we sure as hell don't need the trouble you can bring."

"You can't—"

It happened so fast, T.J. wasn't sure it was actually happening until it was over. The newcomer hit Ricky about five or six times, lightning-quick blows to his stomach and torso. He grabbed Ricky by the scruff of his neck before he could fall and gave him a shove toward the rest of Ricky's gang. The other boys grabbed him and held him upright.

"Do I need to explain this any more?" the black teen-ager asked.

The boys holding Ricky quickly shook their heads. Supporting Ricky, they beat a hasty retreat, the kids standing around making a path for them. Then the black teenager turned to T.J.

"I don't know what that was about," he said, "but I'd just as soon you stayed away from here, too."

T.J. nodded quickly. "Yes, sir," she said. "I will."

He grinned, and a gold tooth gleamed in his mouth.

"'Sir,'" he repeated. "Damn. I don't know that anybody ever called me 'sir' before."

"I didn't mean anything by it."

He nodded. "I know. 'S cool. The name's Terrence."

"Um, it's nice to meet you, Terrence."

Oh God, what a dorky thing to say, she thought as soon as the words were out of her mouth.

"Yeah, I'm sure. Now get out of here."

She gave him another nod and pushed away from the railing and started off in the direction of the mall. The kids stepped aside, making way for her, but before she could get very far, Terrence called after her.

"Yo, girl!"

She paused and turned.

Terrence was still smiling. "I don't know what that dipstick was thinking. Your hat's cool."

"Thanks."

She lifted a hand, then turned again and hurried off, her pulse still drumming far too quickly. God, what a day it had turned out to be. And it wasn't over yet. She still had to meet up with Sheri, find Elizabeth, and then face the music at home, where she was going to be grounded for the rest of her life.

Don't go there, she told herself. One thing at a time.

She was a half dozen lampposts away from where she'd run into Ricky, and almost at the mall, when a voice spoke up from beside her.

"Now, that was lucky. I thought I'd have to step in and give the lad a clap across the back of the head myself."

She stopped dead and looked around, but there was no one there.

"Down here," the voice said.

Her gaze lowered until she saw the strange little man standing beside her on the boardwalk. He wasn't exactly a Little, but he was well under two feet tall.

"Oh, God," she said, and backed away from him.

This couldn't be real.

The little man just watched her as she was brought to a stop by the railing behind her.

Was the weirdness *never* going to end?

"You get away from me," she said.

The little man shook his head. "Oh, please. Look at me. I'm hardly the picture of a viable threat, now am I?"

"How do I know that? For all I know, you could be some demon ninja little man."

"I'm not."

"Then what"—she began, then corrected herself—"I mean, *who* are you?"

The little man made a flourishing bow that would have been comical, except T.J. was wound far too tightly to appreciate the humor.

"I won't be insulted by your asking me what I am," he said. "I'm a gnome. Hedley the Ratcatcher, at your service."

"A . . . gnome . . ."

"Indeed."

A couple walked by, arm in arm, neither of them taking the slightest notice of the little man talking to her.

"They act like they can't see you," she said. She looked around. "Everybody's acting like that."

"Well, we are a secret people," Hedley said. "I took the liberty of moving us a step out of the world where we can see, but not be seen. Hear, but not be heard."

Okay, that didn't sound good at all.

"What do you want from me?" she asked.

"Only your well-being," he assured her. "Your friend Elizabeth asked me to look you up and to tell you that you don't have to worry. She's fine."

"You've seen Elizabeth?"

"I have indeed."

"Where is she?"

"I can't say with one-hundred-percent surety, but right about now she should be approaching the Place of Change."

"I don't understand."

"You know how Littles can change into birds?"

T.J. nodded.

"Well, she's in the company of another Little to have a look at the place where it happens."

"But *where* is it?"

"I couldn't say. It's the apartment of this writer who—"

"Sheri Piper!"

"Yes. Exactly. And—"

"That's where *I'm* going right now."

"Are you, indeed?"

"Come on. We should go and see if we can catch up with her." She started to move away from the railing, then paused. "Unless, um, you're here to stop me?"

"No, no. Let us carry on to the writer's apartment."

So T.J. set off again, this time with a gnome trotting beside her.

"This is so cool," T.J. said as they passed the mall.

They were obviously still invisible to everybody because a skateboarder almost ran right into her. They would have collided if she hadn't jumped aside. Or maybe they wouldn't have. Maybe the skateboarder would have gone right through her.

"Almost being knocked off your feet?" Hedley asked.

"No, silly. The fact that nobody can see us."

"Of course." He waited a beat, then added, "You're taking this rather well."

"Well, after you spend a couple of months hanging out with a Little, you kind of expect the world to be a bit bigger and weirder than most people think it is."

"Of course."

"Hey, how did you find me, anyway?"

"That would be King Rat's doing."

"King Rat?"

Hedley nodded. "Only don't call him that to his face or you'll as much as be naming him your sovereign."

"Now you're losing me."

"It doesn't matter. Just remember it, if you should meet him."

"And he found me?"

"He's an information-gatherer," Hedley said, "with a thousand thousand eyes and ears. Nothing happens that he can't find out."

"That sounds a little creepy."

Hedley shrugged.

T.J. thought for a moment, then asked, "Do those eyes and ears include rats and pigeons?"

"And many more besides."

"I *knew* that bird was checking me out." Before Hedley could ask her what bird, she went on, "So, did you catch him or something?"

"What?"

"Well, you said you're Hedley the Ratcatcher. Did you catch King Rat? Is that why he helped you?"

"It's a bit of misnomer," he explained. "I can talk to rats."

T.J. smiled. "Okay, there's a useful talent."

"And King Rat isn't a rat, per se."

"I think you're losing me again."

"Again, it's not important. But no, I didn't catch him. And he helped me for the price of a pie."

"A pie?"

"He has a sweet tooth. Do you know where we're going?"

T.J. nodded. "We take the next stairs up to Yoors Street. I'm supposed to meet Sheri and Jaime in a coffee shop near her place. It could be a bit of a hike."

"Jaime?"

"He's just a friend."

"Who's also involved."

"I guess," T.J. said. "He hasn't actually *seen* a Little or anything, but he's been helping me out. Here we are," she added as they reached the stairs.

They went up to street level, where T.J. paused to get her bearings.

"Okay, we go that way," she said, pointing to a side street that ran west from Yoors.

She was very careful crossing the street, considering that the drivers wouldn't be able to see her.

"So you said you were a secret people," she said. "Do you mean just gnomes and Littles, or are there others, too?" Then she laughed. "Unless *that's* a secret, too."

Hedley smiled. He pointed to the top of a lamppost across the street. T.J. looked, and her mouth formed a perfect O. There was a little man perched on the crossbeam under the bulb, reading a book.

"Is he another gnome?"

"No, he's a hob. Fairy are as varied and plentiful here as they are anywhere."

T.J. laughed. "I didn't know they were plentiful any-where except in a storybook." A couple of long blocks later, they turned off Yoors Street. She pointed to the neon sign halfway down the block. "That must be the place."

The street was lined with parked cars on either side. At the moment they were the only ones on the sidewalk, though T.J. could see a bag lady pushing her shopping cart down the middle of the street. She kept bending down and feeling under the parked cars with a long stick she carried.

"See," T.J. said, "that's something you'd never see back home."

Hedley nodded. "No, I wouldn't think there'd be many homeless people wandering around in the 'burbs."

"That, too," T.J. said, "but I meant back home in the country, where we moved from this past summer. We don't have homeless people, because if someone falls on hard times, we look after them. Like when my dad's business went belly-up, our neighbors did everything they could to help us before we finally had to give up and move to the jobs my parents got in the city."

"It's not quite the same thing as the community association making sure that undesirables stay off their streets."

"Totally."

They stopped in front of the coffee shop. Looking in, T.J. could see Jaime and Sheri sitting in a booth near the window, but though Jaime was looking right at her, he obviously couldn't see her. T.J. took off her hat and stuck it in her pocket.

"Are we going to stay invisible?" she asked.

"I am—for now," Hedley said.

"Do you want me to get them to come right out?"

He nodded. Then T.J. supposed he did something, because Jaime's eyes suddenly went comically wide. He blinked, then waved to her, but she shook her head and motioned for them to come out and join her.

She watched as they both reached into their pockets to pay for their coffee. Sheri was quicker and laid a couple of bills on the table. Then Jaime was up and hurrying toward the door, Sheri following at a slower pace.

"*Oye*, how'd you do that?" he asked as he came out the door. "Man, you were just *there*, like you came out of nowhere."

Before she could respond, he gave her a hug and added, "Man, you had me worried."

"I had me worried, too."

He let her go suddenly, as though it had occurred to him that he was taking liberties, and stepped back. T.J. wished he hadn't. It was refreshing to have somebody actually happy to see her, and being in his arms had felt good. But she didn't say anything.

"So how did you do that?" Jaime asked. "Just, you know . . . you're *there*." He snapped his fingers.

T.J. turned to look at Hedley. She could still see him, but obviously Jaime couldn't.

"Are you going to show him?" she asked.

"Show me what?" Jaime said, looking around where they stood. "And who are you talking to?"

Then his eyes went wide again.

"Holy crap," he said.

Sheri added a heartfelt, "Oh, my," as she stepped out of the door just in time to see the gnome appear.

"This is Hedley," T.J. said. "He's a gnome."

It seemed an unnecessary elaboration—just looking at him, it was obvious he wasn't human—but then she hadn't known what he was when she'd first met him.

She looked at Jaime and added, "Now do you believe me about Littles?"

"Man, I don't know what to believe anymore."

"Pleased to make your acquaintance," Hedley said, offering them one of his elaborate bows.

Sheri recovered first, but that didn't surprise T.J., seeing as how the author was already familiar with Littles. All Jaime could do was stand there, staring at the gnome, as though the harder he looked, the more it would make sense. If that was his plan, it didn't seem to be working.

"And he's a friend of Elizabeth's," T.J. said, "who, apparently, is on her way to Sheri's house right now."

Sheri nodded. "For the change."

"I'm not sure she actually wants to change," Hedley said, "but she did seem to have a need to actually see where they take place. I'm hoping—"

He was stopped by a car alarm that went off down the street. They all turned to look and saw the bag lady careening down the pavement toward them, her cart squeaking and clattering.

"Good old Pop Can Sally," Sheri said. "She sets off one of those alarms at least once a night."

They saw a door open in one of the townhouses, and a man aimed his car fob at the street. The alarm died and the man went back inside, slamming the door behind him. Pop Can Sally clattered and squeaked her way past them, heading for Yoors Street.

"I hate car alarms," Sheri said. "You'd think they'd have banned them by now. Do they really stop thieves, or are they just there to annoy everybody who lives around you?"

Before any of them could respond, the night was disturbed once more, this time by a flare of light that exploded from under one of the cars near where the alarm had gone off. They were all blinded, and for a moment T.J. thought that the car had literally exploded. Except there was no sound. And as her eyes adjusted once more, stars still flickering in her gaze, she saw that no bits and pieces of exploded car littered the street.

"That was magic," Hedley said.

He started up the street at a run. The rest of them followed, but for all that they had longer legs than the gnome, he quickly left them behind. When they reached the car, Hedley was crouched under the driver's door.

"I'll need some help here," he said. "Go around to the other side and see if you can slide him out—but carefully!"

Him? T.J. thought as the three of them circled to the far side of the car. Him who? And what was he doing lying under a car? And what about the magic?

But when she got to the other side, there was a teenaged boy lying there. T.J. bent down beside the wheel to get a closer look and came face-to-face with—

"Elizabeth!" she cried. "You're safe! God, I've been looking *everywhere* for you."

"And here I am," Elizabeth said, in that dry voice she could use to such good effect. "I could use some help here."

"Holy crap," Jaime said when he bent down beside T.J. "She's real."

"No, I'm a figment of your imagination. Some help?"

Yup, T.J. thought, definitely Elizabeth.

"C'mon," she told Jaime. "Sheri and I will get him from the front and you can push on his legs till we get out from under the car. So who is he?" she added to Elizabeth as they got into position.

"Yeah, and what happened to him?" Jaime asked.

"His name's Jan. He's just this Little who was showing me how to get here."

"A *Little?*"

"He got bigger, okay? Long story. Is he breathing?"

"I think so," Sheri said.

They eased Jan out from under the car until they had him up on the sidewalk. T.J. started to feel a little sick when she could see the blood on the front of his shirt.

"What happened?" T.J. asked.

"That crazy lady hit him with her stick. I think she broke every bone in his chest. And then his head got smashed against the pavement. There was blood coming out of his mouth and he . . . then I . . ."

Sheri pulled the boy's shirt up and ran her hand gently along his ribs.

"He seems okay now," she said.

Elizabeth nodded. "I used my wish—well, technically

Hedley's wish—to make him healthy and Big-sized. I didn't think it had worked, but then everything exploded with light and he was like this. Why won't he wake up?"

"Give him a moment or two," Hedley said.

"Hedley," Elizabeth began.

"It wasn't my wish," he said. "It was Mina's. You know what you've done now?"

Elizabeth nodded. "But I *had* to do it. I couldn't just let him *die*. He didn't even want to come here in the first place."

"I know. We'll work this out."

"Um," T.J. said. "Nobody else has a clue what you're talking about."

"It's not important," Elizabeth said.

"It sounds kind of important."

Elizabeth looked at her, eyes flashing. "Well, it's not. So just forget—"

She broke off when Hedley touched her arm.

"Don't push away those who only mean you well," he said. "T.J. has done nothing but worry and look for you since the two of you were separated."

T.J. expected Elizabeth to snap at him, too. But instead she nodded and took a deep breath.

"You're right," she said. She turned her gaze to T.J. "And I'm sorry. I've just never had someone almost lose their life for me before."

"It's okay," T.J. told her. "I was being too nosy."

Elizabeth shook her head. "No, Hedley's right. You

were being a friend, and I was being my usual a-hole self."

"Are you apologizing?" T.J. asked, a smile twitching in the corner of her mouth. "Because that would be, like, twice now."

Elizabeth laughed, and as she did, T.J. could see some of the tension flow out of her.

"I really missed you," Elizabeth said. "Unlike me, you're a good person."

"Oh, right. You're such a monster."

"I'm sure not perfect."

"And I suppose I am?"

"Closer than me."

"Oh, please. If you knew how many things I screwed up today . . ."

T.J.'s voice trailed off, and the two of them laughed again.

Then, instead of arguing further about who was or wasn't a good person, Elizabeth explained about the wish.

"I don't get the problem," Jaime said. "You just have to do something for this Mina and you're all good, right?"

"I think it's the 'what' that worries her," Sheri said.

Elizabeth nodded. "I mean, she seemed nice and everything, but like Hedley told me before, she's lived her whole life with fairies—so much so that she could almost be considered one."

"And that's bad because . . . ?" Jaime asked.

"Hedley says fairy aren't to be trusted. They're fickle, and you never know what they're going to do or think."

Jaime looked at the gnome. "But he's a fairy, isn't he? I mean, gnomes are a kind of fairy, right? And you seem to trust him."

"Of course I do."

"So what's the——?"

But just then Jan finally stirred. T.J. and Sheri helped sit him up and stayed on either side of him to support him.

"That was . . . weird. . . ." he said. "I was sure I was done for, but I don't feel . . ."

His voice trailed off as he looked around himself, taking in the new size of his surroundings and the strangers around him.

"What the——?"

"It's okay," Elizabeth said.

His gaze went down to her voice, and his eyes filled with bewilderment.

"I'm still dreaming," he said.

Elizabeth shook her head. "No, you're not. You almost died."

"Then . . . then what's happened to me?"

"I had a wish. I knew I had to use it to save your life, but I thought I might as well wish you into a healthy Big instead of just being alive. It looks like it worked."

"Are you feeling all right?" Sheri asked. "No pains, anything?"

"No, I feel fine. I'm just a little confused. Everything's the wrong size." He turned to look around himself. "Who are all you people?"

After introductions were made around, Sheri added, "I

live just across the street. Why don't we get him on his feet and walk him over there?"

Jan shook his head, and a bit of a panicked look came into his eyes.

"No way," he said.

"You can't just sit out here on the pavement all night," Sheri told him, "and it's not as though you'll fit in any of the places you knew as a Little anymore."

"But . . ."

"You need money. You need a place to stay. You need a fresh shirt because the front of that one's all bloody. God, you need I.D., and *how* are you going to get that?"

"I won't go in there," Jan insisted.

"Why not?"

"Because it's the Place of Change."

"But you're not a Little anymore," Hedley said. "It won't affect you."

"I may not be Little-sized, but I'm still a Little. I don't want to take the chance of turning into some weird over-sized bird and then being stuck in that shape."

T.J. tried to imagine one of the birds from the paintings in Sheri's books the size of a human being, then giggled when she did.

"What?" Jan said, turning to her.

"I'm sorry. I was just imagining a bird our size."

"He can stay with me," Jaime said. "We've always got people coming or going in the house. Mama won't mind somebody extra staying for a couple of days, and I've prob-ably got some clothes that will fit him."

"But what about I.D.?" Sheri asked.

"I might be able to hook him up with somebody who can set him up."

"You mean a fake I.D.? No offense, but how would a kid your age know about that kind of thing?"

Jaime shrugged. "I don't. I just know a guy that might."

"That'll have to do," Hedley said.

"And I need to get home," T.J. said. "I am so dead. I'll be lucky if I only get grounded for life. Do you want to come with me, Elizabeth, or . . ."

"Or what?" Elizabeth said.

T.J. nodded with her chin to Sheri's house across the street. "Hedley said you were thinking of trying the change."

"I never said that. I just wanted to look at the place. I think I'm too chicken to actually try it. What I'd really like to do is . . ." She ducked her head a moment, then gave Hedley a quick look. "I think I'd like to take you up on your offer."

"You want to be my apprentice?" Hedley said, obviously surprised.

T.J. was surprised, too.

"You want to be a ratcatcher?" she said.

"No, a baker," Elizabeth said. "That's what Hedley really is. You can't imagine the glorious pies and cakes and cookies he can make."

"Wow," T.J. said. "A baker."

"There's nothing wrong with being a baker."

"Did I say there was? It's just, I don't know, you never

struck me as a baking kind of a girl. But it's cool. I guess you'll be the first punk Little baker."

"Like you'd know."

T.J.'s only response was to pull her hat out of her pocket and put it on.

"Cool hat," Jaime said.

"Yeah," Elizabeth agreed. "I'm impressed. Maybe there's hope for you yet."

"So it looks like everything's worked out," Sheri said.

T.J. shrugged. "Except for being grounded forever when I get home."

"And me not *having* a home," Elizabeth put in.

"I'd offer you mine," Sheri said, "but I get the sense you don't want to try the change."

"No, but the option's always there, right?"

Sheri nodded.

"I can find you a place," Hedley said. "It would have to be near mine, anyway, if you're going to prentice with me, but for tonight, I have a spare room."

"And as for your parents," Sheri told T.J., "maybe I can take some of the heat. Just tell them we got together after the signing—which isn't a lie, really—and that we lost track of time. Here, I'll give you my card. You can have them call me if they want."

"But we should get rolling soon," Jaime said. "*Vámonos ya* and all that."

T.J. stowed Sheri's business card with the one she'd gotten from Red.

"I should get you to teach me Spanish," she told Jaime.

"Anytime."

"And you're going to be okay?" she asked Elizabeth.

The Little nodded. "We'll keep in touch."

"I'd like that, but how will you manage that? You can't exactly pick up a phone."

"We'll figure something out."

Hedley nodded. "We've been doing it for hundreds of years."

So that was how T.J. found herself on the subway going north, sitting on a seat beside Jaime while the two of them watched Jan's utter joy at being a Big. They had the front of the car to themselves. The only other occupants were an old black man sleeping near the back of the car, and a kid too engrossed with his Game Boy to pay them any attention. Jan was wearing a shirt that Sheri had given him.

"First thing," Jan said as he held on to a pole and spun around, "is I'm getting an electric guitar and an amp. A *big* amp. And I am going to make me some *noise*."

"You're going to need money for that," Jaime said.

"So I'll get some."

"You know they put people in jail for stealing, right?"

"So I'll get a job."

"Yeah, but do you have any idea—?"

T.J. gave him a jab in the ribs with an elbow.

"That's cool," she told Jan. "My brother plays in a band."

Jan looked at Jaime. "You see? It's cool. I could be cool."

He went to the front of the car and stared out at the

black tunnel beyond the arcs of the subway car's lights.

"It's like he's totally high," Jaime said.

T.J. nodded. "Sorry about the elbow jab, but I thought he might as well enjoy himself before reality sinks in."

"Yeah, I got that."

They fell silent for a couple of stops. It was enough to just be sitting without some new crisis arriving.

"What are you thinking about?" Jaime asked after a while.

T.J. glanced at him. "It's just weird, Elizabeth apprenticing herself to a baker."

"What's wrong with bakers? You eat bread, don't you?"

"It's not that. It's this whole apprenticing idea. Elizabeth is such a cool, with-it kind of a girl, and apprenticing—it just sounds medieval."

Jaime laughed.

"What?"

"I don't know about the word itself, but the idea's not medieval. It's the way the world works."

"I don't know what you mean."

"Not everybody can afford university. Take my brother Al."

"You have a brother named Al?"

"It's short for Alejandro. The point is, he's working in our uncle Luis's garage, learning the trade from the ground up. He'll be going for his mechanic's license next year. Tio Luis says I can do the same, if I want. I could work in my aunt Marina's restaurant and learn how to cook. Or learn landscaping from my dad." He smiled. "And you were even doing it yourself."

"When was I doing it?"

"When your parents had their farm. Doing your chores was the ground floor to learning how to run the farm."

T.J. nodded. "I guess you're right. Except we don't have our farm anymore."

"Maybe now you can afford university," Jaime said.

"I doubt it. Now that you've explained it, I kind of like this apprenticing idea. But where do you even start with it?"

"That's easy. Like I said, it's the way of the world. You find something you really want to do, then you go find somebody a lot better at it and get them to teach you. You know, they become your mentor."

What would she like to do? T.J. thought. Ride her horse. That's what she'd always loved the best. But it was hard to think of a way you could make a living doing that, and she didn't have a horse anymore anyway.

But she'd always liked messing around with machines. Back home, she was the one who always got the tractor running when it broke down.

That made her think of the biker who'd given her the lift downtown. That motorcycle of his had been so cool. It was like the city equivalent of a flesh-and-blood horse. And that was something you *could* make a living at. Not the riding so much, but what Red was doing. Running a garage that worked on bikes. She wondered if he'd ever thought about getting an apprentice.

Her stop was the end of the line. Jaime and Jan got off at the one before it.

"Are you going to be okay?" Jaime asked as he paused in the doors.

"I doubt it. I think I've had my last taste of freedom until I'm old enough to move out on my own. But at least I'll be able to see you in school."

"Don't let them bully you," he said. "You didn't really do anything wrong." He hesitated, then added, "Well, except for taking off when we saw your dad in the store. But he doesn't know you saw him."

"I guess."

"I . . ." he began, but then he looked too flustered and couldn't seem to continue.

How weird, T.J. thought. She didn't know him well, but for as long as she had, she couldn't remember him ever being at a loss for something to say.

"What is it?" she asked.

"Would you mind . . . could I kiss you?"

T.J. smiled. "I'd like that."

He pressed his lips against hers. She started to lean against him, but then the warning *ting* sounded from the door and he had to get off.

"Tomorrow!" he said as he stepped onto the platform.

Behind him, Jan was turning around and around in a circle, arms spread wide, trying to take everything in.

The door closed and Jaime waved at her, grinning. T.J. was grinning, too.

Tomorrow, she thought as the train pulled out of the

station and she returned to her seat. At least she had something to look forward to.

T.J. called home from the subway station, and her mother came to pick her up because Dad was still en route from the bookstore downtown. Mom seemed more relieved than angry when T.J. got into the car, the anger growing to swallow the relief as they got closer to home. It was Mom anger, which meant it was quiet and pointed, and all the more awkward for that.

Mom was good at this, holding on to a silent anger that made you want to fill up the silence with words. But T.J. knew better than to try. Whenever she did, she always ended up saying things she'd never meant to say. So instead, as they drove home, all she did was tell her story—leaving out the parts about Littles and gnomes, what had happened on the boardwalk and then later on Sheri's street.

"Don't you believe me?" she asked as they pulled into the driveway.

Because Mom had yet to say anything in response.

Mom waited for a long moment, then slowly turned in her seat to look at T.J.

"Of course, I believe you," Mom said. "What I don't know yet are the parts you're leaving out."

Oh, boy.

When Dad got home, they all went into the dining room and sat around the table. Dad at the head, Mom across from him, Derek and T.J. facing each other. It was the same old pine table that had once stood on the linoleum floor in their kitchen back on the farm. Whenever there was a problem, or any kind of trouble, they had a family meeting about it. That was the Moore tradition. The last time they'd had to have one was when Dad told them about how they were going to have to sell the farm.

T.J. had to go through it all again, then Dad told what had happened after they'd gotten the call from Geoff and he'd driven to the bookstore downtown.

Derek was quiet until the end, then he asked, "Is it true what Dad says Geoff told him? That you were saying fairies are real?"

T.J. nodded. "I was just having fun with the idea because of the kind of reading we were going to, but he just went crazy about it. It was scary how crazy he got, and how fast it happened. Before I even knew what was happening, he was refusing to take me to the reading, saying he was going to drive me home. That's why I bolted out of the car."

"You could have called us then," Dad said.

"I should have, I guess," T.J. said. "But I didn't have my cell, and I didn't have change for the phone, and I didn't want to go into the liquor store to get change. And I knew all I had to do was take a bus the rest of the way. It wasn't like you wouldn't know where I was. I really wanted to go to the reading."

Mom shook her head. "Taking the bus like that, all by yourself."

"Mom, kids do it all the time in the city—kids younger than me. The bus and the subway is how they get around."

"But still . . ."

"That doesn't explain why you accepted a ride from this biker," Dad said.

"He wasn't just a biker. I mean, he has a motorcycle, but he owns a garage nearby. He's the guy from the commercial I like, with the horse that turns into a motorcycle."

Her mother smiled. "That is a clever ad."

"I figured I'd be safe, him being a local businessman, and on the TV and all. Anyway, Geoff was freaking me out because he just wouldn't let it go. He was standing there by the bus stop, yelling at me, and the only thing that made him stop was when Mr. Ford asked if I needed help."

Thank God she'd taken the time to check Red's real name from the business card before all of this. Calling him Mr. Ford made him sound so much less like some dangerous biker.

"But he was still a stranger," Mom said. "To simply get on his motorcycle with him . . ."

Dad nodded. "How many times have we warned you about strangers?"

Like, a million, T.J. thought.

"I wasn't going to," she said. "He just offered to stand with me at the stop until the bus came, but then I got scared that Geoff would follow me in his car, so when Mr. Ford asked me if I wanted a ride to the store, I just kind of panicked, I guess, and said yes."

Dad shook his head. "And what about this business at the bookstore? Why would you lie about Geoff like that? Acting like he'd been stalking you for weeks."

"I was just mad at him. He had no right to stop me from going to the reading."

"But to make up such an awful, spiteful story . . ."

"He started it—making up a story about me to the security guard."

Dad sighed. "And what about this Hispanic boy?"

"Jaime."

It was so weird, T.J. thought. If it was a white kid, his ethnicity would never even come up. But if a kid was anything else, some point always seemed to have to be made about the color of his skin, even with people as avowed liberal as her parents.

"Jaime," Dad said. "It sure seems to me like you were planning all along to meet him there."

"I swear I wasn't. He's just a guy I know from school. I ran into him in the store, and he was someone to sit with at the reading."

"I don't know that I like him," Dad said. "He was pretty rude."

"*Really?*"

T.J. was surprised. Jaime had told her that he'd made an effort to be as polite as he could be, considering the circumstances. Cool, and a little distant, but polite.

Dad looked at her, then slowly shook his head. "No, I suppose he wasn't. Not until I went all heavy on him, and even then, he was pretty restrained, given the way kids can talk these days."

T.J. and Derek looked at each other and rolled their eyes.

"Okay, okay," Dad said. "We're getting off topic here. So, after the reading, you went with the author for coffee?"

T.J. nodded. "I'm totally to blame there. I just lost track of time. But she was *so* interesting to talk to."

She pulled Sheri's business card from her pocket and laid it on the table.

"Ms. Piper said you could call her," she added.

"But why didn't *you* call us then?" Mom asked.

"I just didn't think of it. She took me to the subway station and I caught the first train, and then I called you when I got to the station, where you picked me up."

"There's more to this than you're telling," Mom said.

"Well, I could try and remember all the conversations and everything at the reading, if you like."

"Don't get smart," Dad said.

T.J. was feeling bristly. She knew there was more, but how could she possibly tell any of it? It was easier to just get them mad at her for her attitude so that they wouldn't push too hard for more details, because God knew, she'd never been able to get away with telling lies.

But just then Derek put up his hand.

"My turn," he said.

Everyone looked at him.

Dad nodded. Family discussion, so everybody got their say.

"It seems to me," Derek said, "that we should be proud of how T.J. handled the situation with this Geoff guy."

"How do you figure that, son?"

"Well, think about it. I saw him before I left the house

today. He was way bigger than her, and if his abuse had gotten physical, T.J. would have been in real trouble. Now maybe she didn't make the best judgment call with Mr. Ford, but then again, T.J.'s always been a good judge of character—"

"Except for this Geoff boy," Mom said.

"Who both you and Dad vetted," Derek said, "and look how well that went."

Dad nodded. "Point taken."

"Anyway," Derek went on, "I think holding on to this fairies thing until it got to the point it did wasn't the smartest move, but after that, I don't believe she was taking any unnecessary chances. And as for this Jaime . . . I'm just happy she's finally making some friends her own age—he *is* your own age, right?"

T.J. nodded. "Pretty close. He just turned sixteen."

"So my vote is that she gets a stern talking-to—which she's already gotten—and we leave it at that."

"But she should have called," Mom said.

Derek nodded. "But there were circumstances. And don't forget, a lot of the worry and anger you got came from what Geoff told you—not from anything T.J. was doing."

T.J. could only look at her brother. He caught her gaze and winked, and she didn't know what to think. Ever since the swarming incident yesterday, he'd just been so cool. No, scratch that. He was always cool. Now he was cool without also wanting to stick his little sister in a crate and ship her off to some place like Australia.

At either end of the table, Mom and Dad were thinking

over what Derek had said. They must have been communicating telepathically, because they seemed to come to a decision without a word spoken between them. Dad turned to T.J.

"What have you learned from this?" he asked her.

"To always call home as soon as plans get changed."

"Exactly."

"And anything else?"

The words came out before she even realized she was saying them: "And that I want to get a motorcycle."

"What?" Mom said.

Dad shook his head. "Absolutely not."

She looked at Derek, but he just smiled and leaned back in his chair.

God, what had made her come out with that? Things had been going so well. But she was into it now, so she might as well continue. This was, after all, a family meeting, and she knew from when Derek got his driver's license, how this kind of thing was definitely fuel for a family meeting.

"I don't mean right now," T.J. said. "For now I just want to learn how to take care of one. You know, maintenance and safety stuff. I could probably take a course, or an extra class at school in shop."

Her parents simply looked at her, not so much angry as confused.

"For God's sake, *why*?" Mom said.

"Because it's the first thing I've found in the city that comes close to making me feel the way I did when I used to ride Red."

Kissing Jaime had been a close second, T.J. decided, but that wasn't something she was about to share with anyone.

Dad sighed. "You kids have to understand. You only get to play the 'we never wanted to move' card for so long."

"I'm not playing any card," T.J. said. "Now that I've seen that there's more to living here than the 'burbs, I kind of like the fact that we've moved."

"Big ditto over here," Derek chimed in.

T.J. nodded. "I was just explaining why I wanted to get a motorcycle. Probably even a scooter would work."

"But you . . . on a motorcycle," Dad said. "And you want to learn how to maintain it and work on it as well."

"Well," T.J. said, quoting back to her father what he'd told her when she'd first wanted to get a horse, "you can't just own something without knowing how to take care of it properly."

"It's not that preposterous," Derek put in. "Remember, she's the only one who could ever get the tractor running when it broke down."

Mom nodded. "Yes, but . . ."

Derek shook his head. "Oh, Mom, you're not going to say that motorcycles aren't really for girls, are you?"

Mom sighed. "God help me, but yes. That's exactly what I was thinking. Isn't that terrible? After all these years of telling you different."

"It's living in the city," Dad said. "Everything moves so fast, it's all so busy. All our values are being turned around on themselves."

"It's just the opposite," Derek said. "The values we learned living on the farm are what let us cope with the city."

"A motorcycle isn't going to replace Red," Dad said to T.J.

"I know. I just . . ."

T.J. thought about Elizabeth, how even though she was six inches high, she didn't seem to be afraid of anything.

"I guess it's because I know I shouldn't be scared of trying something new," she said.

"But a motorcycle . . ."

"Or a scooter," T.J. added.

Mom and Dad shook their heads, but they did their telepathic-link thing again.

"We'll see," Dad said after a long moment.

T.J. wanted to high-five Derek across the table, but she stayed where she was, hands on her lap. She couldn't believe she'd gotten that much out of Mom and Dad. "We'll see," usually meant they were half-agreed and if you didn't do anything stupid or screw up, the thing you wanted might actually happen. But while she managed to sit still, she couldn't stop from grinning.

Dad cocked an eyebrow and smiled.

"We didn't say 'yes,'" he told her.

"I know."

"Then why do you look so pleased?"

"Because you didn't say 'no,' either."

It was odd, finally getting back to her bedroom. T.J. pulled her new hat from her pocket and tossed it on the end of the bed. Her jacket followed. She went to the window and looked out into the night, marveling that she'd been through as much as she had, yet here she was back in her room once more, safe and sound, and in some ways, nothing much had changed at all.

She turned from the window to see Oscar come sauntering into the room, his tail held high except for the little crook at the end.

Well, one thing had changed.

"No use looking for Elizabeth," she told the cat as he made a circuit of the room, obviously trying to sniff out the Little's new hiding place. "I don't think she'll be back here again."

She hung her jacket on a hook on the back of the closet door, then sat down on the end of the bed. Oscar jumped up and settled on her lap. He started to purr when she scratched him behind the ears.

"Yes, I know," T.J. said. "It's terribly sad that you never got to eat her, isn't it?"

Oscar bumped her hand with the top of his head because she'd stopped patting him.

"Well, *I'm* going to miss her," T.J. said. She stroked Oscar's head. "Yeah, I know. You don't care, do you? Just so long as you get your pats."

There came a *ping* from the direction of her desk. She turned, surprised by the sound until she realized that it was her e-mail program telling her she had new mail.

And I Bid You Good Night

"HOW DO YOU like the room?" Hedley asks.

"It's cool," I say.

And it is, in an old-fashioned, cozy kind of way. Lots of thick carpet, fat-legged antique furniture, drapes and bookcases and old paintings on the walls. But it's weird, too, because of the size issue.

It's not Big-sized, but it's not set up for a Little, either. It's gnome-sized, I suppose, so everything's made to fit someone about four times my height. If I jump, I can pull myself up on the chair by the desk without the need to use my grapple and line, but once I'm up there, I still can't sit at the desk. I can barely peek onto the tabletop, standing on the chair on my tiptoes. The bed's not the giant expanse of a Big bed, but my whole family could easily stretch out on it.

"We'll get some furnishings more suited to your size tomorrow," Hedley says. "And later, when you can afford it, we can find you your own place somewhere away from these suites of mine."

And that's the other weird thing. Fairy hide from Bigs

just like Littles do. But instead of having to make do in the hollows between walls and cramped spaces under floors, they live sort of sideways to the rest of the world. You step through a fairy door, like the one leading into Hedley's home, and it takes you into some little pocket world that takes up no space at all in the Big world.

"No," I tell Hedley. "I'd like the company. I mean, it's not like I know anybody else."

"King Rat can find your family for you."

I nod. "And maybe I'll take you up on that. But first I'd like to get myself settled so that I can, you know, show that I can get along on my own."

Hedley smiles. "I understand perfectly. It's not been that long ago since I moved out of the family home that I can't remember the desire to make my own mark on the world."

I don't know about making a mark—what kind of a mark can a Little leave? And then there's the whole thing about *not* leaving a mark so that the Bigs don't think they've got vermin running around in their house.

But I know what he means.

And I actually like this room. It's warm and cozy, and while the furnishings aren't my size, that's nothing new for a Little.

"So where's the bakery?" I ask.

"There's time enough for that tomorrow as well."

I nod. I get the feeling he's about to go, but I'm not ready to be on my own just yet. I look for something else to talk about, and I don't have to look far.

"What do you think Mina's going to want for the wish?" I ask.

"You don't have to worry about it anymore," he says. "I've decided to take responsibility for it."

"But then *you'll* owe her."

Hedley shrugged. "I can hardly have somebody else lording it over my apprentice, can I? And besides, Mina seems to think the wish was in payment for something she owed me. Let's just leave it at that."

"But what do I owe you?"

"Besides your loyalty as my apprentice? Nothing."

"But . . ."

"Understand, Elizabeth. You did a selfless thing. If you hadn't used the wish—done what you did, when you did—Jan would be dead. But without knowing what it would cost you, you were still willing to take responsibility for the wish and use it to save him. That sort of pluck should be rewarded, not punished."

"I guess. . . ."

He smiles. "Is it so hard to say thank you?"

"No—of course not. I'm totally grateful. For this, and for everything. But it just all seems kind of easy."

"Was it really?"

I think about being kidnapped while hiding in T.J.'s backpack and almost getting eaten by a cat. But I guess, for every scary thing that happened, something good did, too. I had help from Bakro and Mina, and then Hedley. I got to help Jan *and* fulfill his heart's desire to be a Big. I get to make a life for myself, earning my own way.

"Yes and no," I tell Hedley.

He nods, studying me for a moment.

"Are you still thinking about wings?" he asks.

"Honestly, no. If there's anything I want, I'd just like to be able to talk to T.J."

"Well, *that* I can arrange."

He's out the door before I can say a word. A moment later, he's back, laying some kind of electronic device on the carpet where I can just walk over to it. I'm not quite sure what it is. It's about five inches long, three inches wide, and not quite an inch deep. There's a screen, and a small keyboard and some other buttons under the screen. And then I remember all the TV shows Tad and I used to watch. I've seen characters use these things a zillion times. It's a PDA.

"What do you think?" he asks, obviously pleased.

"It's perfect."

Hedley beams. "Small enough for a Little to use, though you can't exactly wander about with it in your pocket the way a Big might. It's got Wi-Fi, so you can access the Internet and do e-mail. You can even use it as a phone, or to text-message."

"You're kidding," I say.

Hedley shakes his head in response, still beaming.

"And I can just use this?"

"That's why I brought it into your room."

"But what are *you* doing with it?"

He laughs. "I might be a gnome, but that doesn't mean I ignore the world around me. If I see something useful, I'm happy to give it a try."

"So, do you have a TV, too?"

He nods. "It's in the study. Do you want to see it?"

"No, I . . ." My gaze goes back to the PDA lying there on the carpet between us. "Can you show me how it works?" I ask.

"Of course."

And that's how, twenty minutes later, I'm sending my first e-mail ever to T.J.'s Yahoo account.

You won't believe where I am, is how I start.

CHARLES DE LINT is widely credited as having pioneered the contemporary fantasy genre with his urban fantasy *Moonheart* (1984). He has been a seventeen-time finalist for the World Fantasy Award, winning in 2000 for his short story collection *Moonlight and Vines*; its stories are set in de Lint's popular fictional city of Newford, as are his novel *The Blue Girl* and selected stories in the collection *Waifs and Strays* (a World Fantasy Award Finalist).

He has received glowing reviews and numerous other awards for his work, including the singular honor of having eight books chosen for the reader-selected Modern Library "Top 100 Books of the Twentieth Century."

A professional musician for over twenty-five years, specializing in traditional and contemporary Celtic and American roots music, he frequently performs with his wife, MaryAnn Harris—fellow musician, artist, and kindred spirit.

Charles de Lint and MaryAnn Harris live in Ottawa, Ontario, Canada—and their respective Web sites are www.charlesdelint.com and www.reclectica.com.